CW01464980

# BAD KITTY

ELIZA GAYLE

GYPSY INK BOOKS

# BAD KITTY

## A SOUTHERN SHIFTERS NOVEL

Copyright By ELIZA GAYLE © 2013
All Rights Reserved

Published by
Gypsy Ink Books

eliza@elizagayle.com
http://ElizaGayle.com

# A NOTE FROM ELIZA

When Kitty first showed up in the second book of the Southern Shifter series (MATE NIGHT) I never envisioned her as more than a barely there minor character. Then she showed up again in the third book of the Southern Shifter series (ALPHA KNOWS BEST) and I started to get the idea she wasn't going away. It took a while to get her story out of her but I'm excited it's here and I get to share with all the readers who've patiently waited for another sexy shapeshifter book from me.

Happy Reading

Eliza

P.S. For those fans of the free short story White Cougar Christmas who haven't yet made it to the full story of Dean and Nikki (BE WERE), you might get excited when you read Bad Kitty. There's a little tidbit just for you! However, Dean and Nikki's book is now available and immediately follows Bad Kitty in the reading order.

# Acknowledgments

There are many people who go into making each book the best it can be. Editors, cover artists, beta readers, critique partners and good friends. I owe them all so much.

Thanks to the patience and help of Cat Johnson, Dahlia Rose and my family, I was able to finish this book and they helped me make it even better.

Special thanks to the beta readers Patricia Slovinsky, Tina Dale, and Lisa Morgan who took the time to read from one chapter to the entire book and provide their opinion on how the story was going. Your input was invaluable.

# CHAPTER ONE

Kitty stared down at the keys in her hand and shook her head. Walking away from the Clan and everything she'd ever known had been hard enough, but this...this was too much. She wasn't just some damn charity case Kane could sweep under the rug by offering an empty house in the neutral zone for her to live in. Her entire life to this point had been in the sheltered protection of her clan. Now they didn't want her, just like her father.

Anger boiled in her veins every time she thought of him. She tried to do the right thing when she found out about his attempt to kidnap Malcolm's child, but the Clan decided her efforts were too little too late. Her father's attempts to kill or undermine the

Guardian brothers at every turn had failed. He'd been a damned fool all along. Yes, she'd remained quiet despite what she knew. But she didn't need to stick her neck out and bring her own father's wrath down on her head.

All she'd had to do was wait for everything to blow up. And there lay the crux of her problem today. She'd had more than a pretty good idea about much of what her father was up to and had kept the information to herself. As far as she'd been concerned, it hadn't been her place to either agree with him or stand against him.

The why of most of his schemes still escaped her, so she ignored the havoc he'd created. She'd been under the mistaken impression that, somewhere deep down, her father cared about her. But then she'd discovered the child. Her father found out about Malcolm's secret offspring and had planned to do who knows what with her. So she'd snuck the child away and out of her father's reach. Rescuing the girl had been her only saving grace with the council and meant the difference between a death sentence and *this*. At the last minute Kane had stood up for her and offered a compromise in the form of an extended vacation. Kitty chuffed, the sound far more animal than human.

*Vacation my ass.*

More like indefinite exile, and to the neutral zone no less. The only people who belonged here were the half-breeds no one knew what else to do with. Kitty curled her upper lip, pushed opened the door and exited the car packed with the few belongings she'd been allowed to keep. She headed toward the small cottage with the extended wrap-around porch. Maybe, just maybe, if she'd been offered a place like this on clan land, its pretty exterior would have charmed her. But here it was no more than a prison of four walls where she'd have to hide from the local residents. No one wanted a full blood feline hanging around. Trust would be impossible.

She had half a mind to take her chances with the humans instead.

The sun's rays trickled through the tree canopy that offered the hideout more privacy than she'd expected. Despite the chill in the late afternoon air, everything around her mocked her with its almost summer like beauty. She didn't want to notice the pretty poppies growing in a border around the left side of the yard, nor did she want to see raised garden beds at the edge of the property that beckoned for someone to fill them with fruits and vegetables.

They could dress it up and call this place whatever they wanted. She'd essentially been kicked out with no information about when or if she could ever return. Irritated and tired, she walked up the driveway toward her banishment. As far as she knew the place had stood empty for many years. While Deals Gap, North Carolina had officially been declared a neutral zone in the tenuous treaty between the wolf and cougar clans, they'd been encouraged to keep to their own lands as much as possible. Especially her. Her father had been beyond vigilant in his preaching about keeping the bloodlines pure and not associating with other races for anything more than absolute necessity. Supposedly everything he'd done had been in some part due to his bloodline obsession. Although, considering her recent discovery of a half-sister who was half-cougar and half-witch, she'd begun to question everything.

Kitty rubbed her head and tried to push the anger and resentment from her thoughts. Her actions of the last few years had not been great either. The embarrassment of her relentless pursuit of a man who didn't give a rat's ass about her burned through her soul like acid. Unfortunately there were a lot of other things she'd done almost as humiliating as her behavior with Kane. Things she couldn't take back or change.

She'd hole up here for a few weeks until she got her head on straight and come up with a new strategy for the next several months. Her father's assets had all been confiscated, leaving her with nothing to fall back on. Her job skills were a joke and there had been no reason to hold down a nine to five with her father taking care of everything. Kitty had wasted all her time being a stuck up bitch. There, she admitted it.

Oh, how the mighty have fallen...

Stepping onto the small porch, Kitty lifted the sunglasses from her eyes. The paint looked fresh and the area around her was neat, obviously someone took care of the place. As she slid the key into the deadbolt of the door, the scrape of metal on metal screeched through her head. She pushed the door open and the air suddenly shifted around her. The hair at her nape stood on end. Tension pulled at her skull and instantly notified her she was no longer alone. Before she could react, or even turn around, the door slammed in her face and she flew backwards. Her muscles flexed and her claws burst free as she scrambled to catch herself.

The air whooshed from her lungs as her thickened nails dug into the wooden steps of the porch, barely breaking her fall. She pushed to her feet at the same time a hard kick was delivered to her ribs and another to her face.

"Don't even think about it, bitch. You've had this coming for a long damn time and I'm going to make sure you finally get what's yours."

Black spots blurred Kitty's vision from the pain of the blows. She didn't need sight to put a face to that voice. Laurel James had been gunning for her for a very long time. Competition among the feline women for the men of their kind was fierce and often violent. This wouldn't be the first time she'd fought for what she wanted.

As Kitty perched precariously on all fours, several pairs of legs crossed her line of sight. Laurel wasn't alone. Whatever they had planned, she'd brought reinforcements and this wasn't going to go well for

Kitty. It didn't take a genius to realize she'd been out maneuvered and out numbered. Now her only thought turned to survival as she struggled to find a solution before they pulled her limb from limb.

"This is your idea of a fair fight? Four against one?" Kitty spat. She needed to try and buy some time. She'd dropped her keys and she needed precious seconds to locate them.

"What the hell do you know about fair? You have dicked around with our men behind our backs, done everything in your power to hold us back in clan politics, all while you schemed with your father to bring down our Guardians. Our only protection from the mongrels across the state line. And if that wasn't enough, just when you were finally due to get what you had coming, you somehow convinced Kane to have mercy on you and were given this cozy little house to hide out in."

White-hot rage filled Kitty's veins. She fought through the pain and pulled herself upright. With one eye on Laurel and the other on her pack of stupid bitches, she slowly took a step forward. "Are you on drugs? Do you honestly think coming here was some kind of reward? I've lost my father," she pointed her finger at Laurel, who inched back a few steps. "I've lost my home. And now I'm being forced to look at your ugly face."

Laurel's face turned various shades of red and Kitty swore steam came from the woman's ears. It dawned on her that she might have pushed too hard when the four of them circled her in a show of solidarity. She frantically searched the area for her keys with no luck. They had to be here. They couldn't have just—

"Looking for these?" Laurel held up the keys Kitty had been hunting for. "Your overconfidence is astounding." She circled Kitty. "But that's okay because before we're through you're going to wish you were dead instead of exiled."

"Shut the fuck—" Kitty's head snapped back as Laurel slapped her across the cheek. Tears she refused to shed burned in her eyes. No matter what happened she would never give these women the satisfaction they sought.

"Is that the best you've got? Fighting like a girl?" This time the hit came from someone else and knocked her into the porch railing. Pain exploded in her head and immediately her ears began to ring. She tasted blood.

"I've waited a long damn time for this so you're going to listen to every word I have to say."

*To hell with that.* Kitty tuned out Laurel and battled to her feet, only to be slammed to her knees. Fear shot through her mind as the true state of her predicament sank in. They were going to kill her. Her last moments would involve a handful of catty women out for revenge and an ordinary house in the middle of the neutral zone. Her heart sank. How had things gotten to this point? All her life she'd followed her father's rules, even clan rules for the most part. The fact she used her father's power to cause havoc now and again seemed minor in comparison to this. The taste of bitterness irritated her tongue. Didn't she deserve better?

"For years you've used your perfect face and perfect body to get whatever it was you wanted. What would you do if that were no longer an option? Would you simply find another way to make people suffer? Or would you turn into your father?"

Kitty didn't want to listen to this. She'd only done what she had to. No more, no less. How exactly did that make her so much different than everyone else who was looking out for themselves?

"Jealousy doesn't become you, Laurel. You should know that by now."

Another blow to her ribcage toppled Kitty to her side, knocking the wind out of her again. That one came from what suspiciously felt like a fucking baseball bat. She couldn't keep taunting them if this was how they were going to respond. She'd be dead in minutes. She had to think.

"Aww, poor Kitty. You have no idea do you?"

The venom in Laurel's words unnerved Kitty. Her former childhood friend appeared to be hanging on to sanity by a thread.

Kitty tried to get up, but Laurel grabbed her wrist and pushed her down. "You think this one little tiny mark is punishment enough?" Laurel pressed painfully into the neutral zone brand on her wrist. "That being magically labeled as an outsider is enough to make up for all the torment and suffering you've caused? Yeah, you have no idea. But I'm going to show you. An eye for an eye, right?"

Laurel crouched down and entered Kitty's line of sight. Her anger twisted the woman's normally pretty face into an ugly scowl.

"I never meant to—"

Laurel twisted Kitty's wrist to the breaking point, making her scream. "Don't even bother. An apology now would mean nothing. But this..." Laurel stretched her free hand in front of Kitty's face and extended her claws. "This is what we call a proper payback."

Kitty's old friend swiped those lethal claws across the left side of Kitty's face, slicing into her flesh. The scent of blood filled the air and for one stunned second, Kitty went numb. Then the searing pain of burning from the inside out sliced through her. She tried to breathe and couldn't. Pain so intense robbed her of any semblance of coherency. Her eyes opened wide and she looked at the woman she'd once called friend as the shock of what she'd done sank in.

"That's right, little miss Kitty, it fucking burns doesn't it? Trust me, it's about to get a whole lot worse."

From behind her someone tore through her shirt and clawed at her back, arms and legs. From some dim part of her brain, Kitty registered the screams tearing through the air as she thrashed in their grip, frantic for escape. The stench of burning flesh mixed with blood filled her head as she fought wildly for freedom. Fire crawled along her entire body, getting worse the harder she fought. When Kitty's brain began to shut down, the animal inside her took over and fought for survival, clawing its way to freedom.

An idea popped into her head. Maybe there was a small chance.

"Enough," Kitty screamed. "Just kill me. Please," she begged. "Just do it. For the love of God do not make me listen to any more of your insane drivel."

The blow she'd been hoping for came in the form of a right cross to her jaw, knocking her on her ass. She prayed for a blackout that never came. The pain, however, exploded in her head so fierce she couldn't draw a breath. With her mind reeling, she almost didn't notice when the hands holding her down broke free.

A glimmer of hope threaded through the pain. She swiveled her head and met Laurel's gaze. The smug look did her in.

With the last burst of strength she could gather, Kitty charged her, moving as fast as possible before the others had a chance to stop her. Together they slammed into the side of the house with Laurel's head taking the brunt of the blow. Someone came at her from behind, punching Kitty in the side of the head so hard she saw stars. Thankfully, she managed to keep a hold on Laurel. Kitty kicked and snarled at the others as she tried to fight them off.

A fierce growl erupted from Laurel that turned into a high-pitched scream. Kitty froze for a second before she was thrown backwards. She twisted to land on her feet but failed. Her shins skidded across the rocks in the garden, tearing through her pants and digging into her skin. The burning across her face and body felt like she'd been doused in gasoline and set on fire. This was it. Her one and only chance. Kitty dug deep for every ounce of energy she could muster until her skin tingled and bones popped.

"Shit. She's changing. Hurry, grab her!"

Kitty ignored the commotion behind her and twisted to her hands and feet mid shift. Her clothes shredded and the excruciatingly painful shift finished in a blur. By some miracle she probably didn't deserve, she was free. Already in motion, she ran for the woods behind the house. Escaping into the cover was her only chance. Cats yowled behind her, letting her know the rest of the women had shifted and were likely in pursuit.

The shift had spent more energy than she could afford but adrenalin pushed her onward. She didn't want to die like this. Once under the canopy of trees she didn't slow her pace to give them any chance to catch up. Every advantage she possessed due to her DNA was mirrored in those who chased her. She ran over rocks, roots and natural crevices until her lungs burned and she wanted to vomit. It was difficult to hear anything over the blood rushing in her ears and her heart racing. She pushed on without looking back or letting up for even a second.

When she splashed through the first river she ached to stop and drink. A new luxury she couldn't afford. The pads of her paws had split and cracked ages ago, or at least many miles behind her. When the sun finally dipped down below the horizon Kitty couldn't take another step. Nothing she'd tried had doused the fire under her skin. She slowed her pace and ducked behind a large boulder to shift and gather her strength. If they caught her, so be it. She already felt like she'd been thrown from a cliff, might as well go for the real thing. Maybe she'd get a chance to take one or two of them with her. Kitty snarled with anger so strong it ached in her bones.

Her chest heaved as she collapsed against the cool surface of hard rock. Everything ached, from head to toe. And despite the shift, which should have helped her heal, her skin still burned out of control. Through sheer desperation, she stilled her body and listened for signs of the others. Nothing but deafening silence met her ears. Even the small wildlife sensed a dangerous predator and moved on. At this point she didn't care if they found her. She'd gladly choose death if it meant the end of this agony.

Never in her life had she traveled this far by foot. Glancing around all she saw were the same trees and dirt that covered the region, but there were no obvious signs of where she'd ended up. With the moon about to rise, she'd been running so long she had to have left the neutral zone hours ago. There were only two possible locations, one of which put her in more danger than the people chasing her.

Curious about the whereabouts of the women who wanted her dead, she peered from behind her hiding spot. To her surprise, there was no one around. Either they'd given up at some point or they were lying in wait for her to shift. Speaking of... Kitty noticed her paw and front legs shaking from the effort of holding this form. With her energy this depleted she had no choice, she couldn't hold the magic another second. A wave of energy flashed over her and her cougar body disappeared to be replaced by her now bruised and battered human form.

Unlike the other shifters in her clan, her feline form was not an equal state. Without the energy to maintain the cat, she automatically shifted back to her human form. She had no idea what it meant, but instinct cautioned her to keep her anomaly a secret. Not even her father knew about this strange quirk. He'd had a long list of reasons why she failed him as his offspring, he didn't need another.

It was quickly growing dark and she desperately needed shelter, and a doctor. Unfortunately she had nothing left, energy wise, to move. The chill in the night air raised goose bumps on her arms and legs. Maybe a few hours more of this and she'd die of exposure and whatever poison they'd forced on her. Exposure sure as hell beat getting ripped to pieces by a group of she cats out for revenge. Sensitive bitches. Nothing she'd ever done to them warranted a death sentence.

Without a stitch of clothing left to cover with, she'd never make it through the night. She needed the cat to get her through this. Kitty focused inward and reached for the elusive animal and the magic that made her who she was. A slight twinge in her legs and arms made her hold her breath. Maybe...

She focused and concentrated, dug deep and willed the change. Nothing happened. Shit out of luck.

Her only hope of survival at this point would be human medical attention. She was quite certain a few of her ribs were cracked and she would be surprised if she didn't need some stitches to sew her back together again. Hell, even a hot bath might coax the cat to heal her.

However, the constant burn under her skin really worried her. What the hell had those women used on her? So much for the quiet and boring exile Kane offered her. Bitterness burned almost as much as the vile poison.

She laughed out loud, a twisted and dark sound that should have frightened her. If she had enough energy left for fear.

"Well, well. What do we have here?"

Kitty jerked at the sound of the voice behind her. The automatic instinct to move and hide left her writhing in more agony. *Fuck!* She wasn't going anywhere.

A man—no—she sniffed the air—several men moved closer, forming a tight circle around her resting place. Not human. Kitty bared her teeth and snarled.

"I thought you said you smelled a dead cat, Bobby. She don't look dead to me." He paused, looking her over from head to toe. "She does look a bit like a used up chew toy though."

"That's okay. Either way she don't belong on our land. Her trespassing gives us the right to do whatever we want with her."

Kitty shivered and forced her body to turn and face all of the newcomers who stunk to high heaven. God, didn't they know how to bathe? That slight movement forced a new eruption under her skin. Her mouth opened to tell them exactly what she thought of that idea and instead a scream erupted.

"Jesus Christ. Shut her up. What the hell kind of noise is that?"

One of the men rushed forward and clamped his hand over her mouth. In automatic survival mode now, she bit him. He reared back and she screamed again before he backhanded her, sending her flying across the clearing and into a tree. She fell to the ground with a painful, heavy thud. Black spots blurred her vision again as she tried to gather some shred of willpower to get up and fight. Again, nothing happened.

"Here kitty, kitty, kitty. You don't have to snarl at us and play hard to get. I think you're going to like us. Maybe if you play nice and do your job well, we'll let you live—for now."

Bile rose in her throat as the three men approached her. She closed her eyes against their faces as a massive surge of fear gripped her insides.

*Please let me die. Please let me die. Please let me die. Anything else but this. Please.*

She knew her prayers would go unanswered so she did the next best thing she could. She used the fear, pushed through the pain and agony ripping through and struggled to her feet. The men before her grew blurry. The forest spun around her. Her legs shook and she held out her arms to keep balanced. A loud noise drew her attention, but her eyesight had worsened. The black edges around her vision were growing larger and all she could make out were fuzzy images in front of her. It was impossible to hear anything over the blood now roaring in her ears.

She couldn't move, she couldn't speak and now she couldn't see. Finally her knees buckled underneath her and she gratefully succumbed to the darkness sucking her in. It was all she had left.

R afe Comyn entered the clearing a second before the battered and broken woman collapsed. He tempered his instinct to run to her assistance. The three men from his pack who surrounded her were not his favorite people and rushing them would send them on the attack. This was not going to go well.

"What the hell is going on here, Tanner?" Rafe demanded.

All three men turned his way and snarled. Their faces were already elongated from a partial shift, their arms and chests covered in fur. Saliva dripped from their mouths and for a second Rafe's stomach turned. They looked more like a rabid group of dirty animals instead of the superior wolf shifters they were supposed to be. The half beast form wasn't the most attractive to begin with. On these three, it was downright nasty.

"This is none of your business, Rafe. We found her first so back off." The gruff voice of the wolf made the human hard to understand.

"Yeah, I can see that. You've cornered a woman and beat her half to death. That's really something to be proud of."

The largest of the group broke rank and moved toward Rafe. "We haven't touched her yet. We found her like this, and she ain't no woman. She's a feline bitch."

Rafe eased forward, making sure to not make any sudden movements. He could take on Tanner and his friends if he had to, but he might as well try and be diplomatic first. The Alpha wouldn't take kindly to him starting a fight and right now pack politics were tense at best. A quick glance at the woman showed her passed out on the ground, but her chest rose and fell just enough for him to see she indeed still lived.

"Then why the hell do you look like wild animals about to attack? Are you planning to eat her?" He knew exactly what they were going to do with her.

"We're about to claim her."

Great, just what he thought. They were stupid *and* horny, his favorite combination. Not. Rafe fought the urge to roll his eyes against the cliché of these men. Not just men though. They were pack, which offered a whole host of complications he was about to step into.

"She's in no condition to be claimed. From what I can see she's barely alive." He brushed past Tanner and knelt beside the woman, ignoring the warning growls behind him. He bent down and sniffed her from head to toe. The wolf's keen sense of smell would tell him everything he needed to know. "She needs immediate medical attention."

"Nuh huh. What do we care if she's hurt? She's one of them. All the woman has to do is shift again and she'll be fine."

Rafe seriously doubted that was the case. In this condition her body should have already reverted to the cougar he scented inside her. There was something seriously wrong here. He pressed his

25

fingers to her neck to check for a pulse and nearly jumped out of his skin. An electric jolt fired across his flesh, making the hairs on the back of his neck stand on end. *Good God.*

He peered closer for a better look. The red streaks in her long blonde hair appeared to be dried blood and the swelling on her cheek and eye were already turning colors. Not to mention the vicious cut bisecting half her face. Someone or someones had certainly given her one hell of a beating. He turned and glared at the men behind him. If not Tanner and his ugly friends, then who? She was too far into their territory to simply be lost. He ground his back teeth, knowing these idiots had found her first, giving them rights to claim her.

His wolf growled inside him, a low but distinct warning. He did not like that idea one bit.

Reluctantly he turned his back to the woman and faced the three men. It wouldn't work well to appear overly interested in her. One whiff of his interest and this situation would turn violent in a heartbeat.

"Her pulse is faint, I don't think there's going to be a claiming here tonight. She can't shift if she isn't conscious. I'm taking her to doc for medical attention, although I'm not even sure she'll live. She smells like death.

"Now wait just a minute." Tanner moved forward.

Rafe held up his hand to halt the other man and growled deep and loud, making sure to thread the noise with the full strength of his dominance. All three men looked up at him in shock. "You ready to challenge me, Tanner? I know you've been dying to do something, but I doubt this is what you had in mind."

"But we found her, so we've got rights. You can't stop us. It's the law!" The three men took a tentative step in Rafe's direction.

"I'm not kidding here. One more step and I'll take it as a personal challenge. It's been a while since I've ripped out anyone's throat, so I'm due."

They froze, each looking back at the other. Finally Tanner shrugged and stepped from in front of Rafe's path. "This ain't over. We aren't just giving up our rights to her. You can have her for now, but we'll be coming for her soon."

The menace in Tanner's voice wasn't lost on Rafe. What he'd really meant was that after he gathered a few more people to his side, he'd be ready for the challenge. This was what an alpha wolf on the rise had to deal with on a regular basis. If you couldn't prove your dominance, then you had no business becoming a leader.

"Anytime, Tanner, anytime."

Rafe turned and scooped the woman from the dirt. She barely stirred. He seriously wondered if she'd live. The cuts on her skin looked like slashes from claws and they were ugly, but turning darker way too fast. Those were no ordinary wounds.

Despite her battered condition, he sensed an inner strength that appealed to his wolf. It left him with an almost uncontrollable urge to lay her out and nestle his nose against her unmarred flesh. The underlying fragrant scent of a woman managed to get in his head through the harsher smell of whatever had been done to her. To his horror, his body hardened as her scent imprinted on his brain. It was time to get them both out of here.

He brushed past the men before any of them changed their mind. He knew the woman in his arms needed more urgent care than they realized. Fortunately, he wasn't far from his cabin and his cell phone. How she made it this far in without setting off any alarms surprised the hell out of him. Not that he doubted for a second Tanner and his crew would spread the word faster than wildfire. If Rafe was lucky, he'd make it to nightfall before the Alpha came calling.

## CHAPTER
# THREE

O ne hundred yards from Rafe's home the woman in his arms stirred. Her eyes fluttered open and her vivid green gaze latched on to him.

"Who are you? Am I dead?"

"Doesn't matter and not yet. Save your energy because I think you're going to need it."

"What happened?" she asked. "Where are we going?"

Rafe smiled at the irritation in her weak voice. "I was hoping you could tell *me* what happened." She slipped in his grip and he tightened his arms around her.

She briefly squeezed her eyes shut but not before he saw the flash of pain in her gaze. Her mouth opened on a pant. "There were three men," she wheezed. "I thought they were going to kill me."

"If only you'd been that lucky."

Her eyebrows drew together in question.

"They wanted a lot more than your death, at least at first."

He watched her facial expression change the moment she understood what he was saying. She immediately struggled in his arms, which he stifled by tightening his grip. He hated hurting her further, but much more of this and she'd make things far worse.

"Put me down. You—you—" she cried out at the pain her writhing had stirred.

Rafe smiled down at her despite the serious situation. "I don't think you're in any position to fight with me, cat girl. Relax and let me get you some help."

Narrowing her eyes, she managed a vicious little glare through the swelling of her face and eye. The edges of her gash were already black and beginning to fester.

"Down, girl. In a minute we'll be at my cabin and we can see about getting you patched up." And he could get her out of his arms where the soft brush of her skin teased him mercilessly. Her lack of clothing left nothing to the imagination and that pulled at him much more than it should. He should be shot for the filthy thoughts running through his head. She was seriously injured and he was thinking wildly inappropriate ways to get what he wanted from her.

"Where exactly are we?" She tried to turn her head to see in front of them and hissed sharply at what he imagined was a move that must have hurt like fucking hell.

"Deep into where you aren't supposed to be, I'm afraid." He carried her up the steps to his cabin and held her on one arm so he could open the door. "I'd welcome you to my home, but I doubt there's going to be much of a welcome for you."

She turned and met his gaze. "What does that mean?"

"Do you know where you are?" he asked.

Her eyes widened a little as she realized. "I don't have to know, I can still smell...wolf territory."

Rafe shrugged. "We'll worry about that later." He carried her straight to the extra bedroom and laid her on the bed. She cried out when he jostled her.

"Sorry." The scent of her pain filled the small room and mingled with the strange odor he'd detected on her earlier. He grabbed the extra blanket from the foot of the bed and covered her as quickly as he could. Not before he got a good look at dark, pink nipples atop her generous breasts. He even noticed the large freckle dotting one of them. To his eternal shame, his mouth watered as her lush body disappeared behind the bulky blanket. What the fuck was wrong with him?

"I'm going to ruin your bed," she murmured. Her face had turned two shades of grey since he'd jostled her onto the mattress. The last thing on his mind was the ruination of his furniture.

"Not my bed. And I can get another one easy enough."

"Need a shower," she whispered.

Rafe leaned in and brushed the hair from her face, easing the red streaked blonde hairs from the wound on her left cheek so he could get a better look. "You have bigger things to worry about besides ruining furniture and a shower. First I'm calling the doc and then we'll see about getting you cleaned up."

"But—"

"Don't bother, lady. You're in no position to argue at this point." Now irritated with his behavior, Rafe left the bedroom and scooped his cell phone from the kitchen counter. He didn't like the way the cat woman made him feel or the thoughts running rampant through his mind. Even more worrisome were her injuries. Why the hell hadn't she shifted to let the cat heal her?

He punched in the memorized phone number and waited for someone to answer. On the third ring he got a gruff hello.

"Hey, Doc. I need your help."

His friend groaned. "Why do you insist on calling me that? You know I hate it."

Rafe laughed. "I know. That's why I do it."

"Clearly you don't really need my help. So if you don't mind I'm going back to—"

Rafe straightened, frustration setting in. They didn't have time for this. "Look this is serious. I have a situation that needs immediate medical attention."

He listened while Doc moved around and whispered to someone that he was sorry but he had to go before he responded. "Okay I'm up and on my way. I'll be there in ten minutes. But maybe you should give me a heads up on what I'm walking into."

Oh boy. "I've got a shifter that's been shredded to hell and back. There are cuts across half her body that aren't healing and turning black at the edges. I think she's dying."

"Her?" Doc asked.

"Yeah, why is that important?"

"The fairer sex is always important," his friend replied.

"Whatever, dude. Get your head out of your pants and get the hell over here."

"You take all the fun out of an emergency situation, Rafe."

Rafe ignored his friend's attempt at drawing him out. "Well, that's not all." He took a deep breath and blurted it out. "She's not wolf."

"Jesus, Rafe. What have you stepped into?" He had his attention now. "Seriously, man. Are you telling me you have a half dead *cat shifter* in your possession?"

Rafe pushed his fingers through his hair. "Well, when you put it that way..."

"Fuck!" A car door slammed. "Make it five minutes."

Rafe ended the call and tossed the phone to the couch. During the call he'd paced across the living room and now found himself outside the bedroom door listening to the feline's breathing. Shallow breaths followed by a series of whimpers came from her every minute or so. He ached to go in and try to comfort her but he sensed he was already too deep with this one. If he went back in he'd only touch her again and she needed to be one hundred percent off limits to the likes of him.

The charge he'd felt when they'd touched earlier still unnerved him. One word had whispered through his brain, one he adamantly refused to acknowledge. No freaking way was this happening to him now. As far as he knew, this strange woman was at death's door. The smell of it still cloaked the room. Hell, the entire house. *If Doc couldn't help her...*

The beast inside him snarled. Those were thoughts he couldn't afford to entertain. He was on the cusp of becoming the pack Alpha and he'd all but dared Tanner to challenge him for it. Maybe he needed his head examined. Yeah, when Doc got done fixing up the girl, he could check him out too. Rafe laughed. *Yep, losing it.*

A car door slammed out front, pulling Rafe from his errant thoughts. One sniff of the air and he knew help had arrived. He'd know his best friend and Omega's scent anywhere. He'd have some explaining to do, but first he needed Simon to save her. He had a very bad feeling that if he didn't there was more at stake than a simple stranger's death.

Simon rushed through the door without knocking. He entered the room a bit wild eyed and disheveled. Rafe lifted one brow. "Rough day?"

"Smart ass. Don't give me that. You know exactly what I was doing when you called with your urgent drama."

"My drama?" Rafe narrowed his eyes.

Simon grinned despite the tension in the air. "Never mind, where is she?"

"Spare bedroom."

He went inside the room and Rafe fell in behind him. The low whistle from his friend didn't make him feel any better.

He lifted the blanket and got a good look at the damage. To Rafe's surprise, she didn't stir as Simon began to touch her.

"She's out cold. How long has she been like this?"

"She was awake ten minutes ago if that's what you mean, but I don't know when she got hurt. I found her in the woods like this maybe thirty minutes ago. Tanner and his buddies had found her and were about to claim her."

Another low whistle. Doc was beginning to get on his nerves.

"You took her from Tanner? He gave her up willingly?"

"Yeah, and no." He bristled at the tone of Simon's question. This wasn't about him and Tanner. His friend only needed to be worried about the woman. "Can you help her?"

Doc leaned over and pressed gently at the wound on her face. "I don't know. These are not simple cuts. See that discoloration around the skin?" He pointed to the black, rippled edges Rafe had noted earlier.

"Yeah."

"That's not natural. I hate to say this because I think your life is about to get too complicated, but I think she's been poisoned." Doc bent over and placed his nose close to the wound on one of her arms and sniffed. "Not sure what it is yet though. Smells a little like sulfur but there's something else I don't recognize."

Rafe nodded. He'd expected as much. "What do you need me to do?"

"Get the bigger bag out of the trunk of my car. I'm going to need some strong stuff to counteract whatever she's been hit with." He looked up. "With this much damage, why the hell is she still in human form. Her body is raging with fever. She needs the animal."

"I've already had the same thought. Aren't all cougars and wolves the same in their shifting patterns? Isn't it automatic for them too?"

Doc looked up at him. "Yeah. They shift the same as us. At least they're supposed to."

Rafe didn't like the implications in his friend's words. The more he learned, the more complicated the situation became. He walked away without responding, but the heaviness settled into his chest. If the damned felines had differences they didn't know about, then there was no telling what else they were hiding. And that damned peace treaty they'd signed was already on shaky ground. Lately there'd been a lot of activity on both sides that made keeping the peace all the more difficult, especially in the neutral zones. Violence had escalated in the last several weeks between the wolves, felines and the others.

More and more half-breeds were popping up and they didn't like being segregated from their families. With the female wolf population lower than ever, the pack had again begun grumbling about the issues. Rafe rubbed his forehead, hoping he could stave off the coming headache a bit longer. He and Doc had some ideas and if they could make it through the next couple of weeks without trouble, they might get a chance at implementing some of them.

Rafe retrieved the medical supplies from Doc's car and returned to his meager guest bedroom. The bedclothes had been stripped from his guest and he heard the sound of running water coming from the adjoining bath.

"Help me get her in the tub. First thing we've got to do is get the fever down."

Rafe left the bag at the end of the bed and nudged his friend aside. He gingerly picked up the woman and cradled her to his chest. He took care to not touch the areas he suspected were infected.

Surprisingly, she didn't stir.

"I've given her a sedative that should keep her out for a while. I can't imagine the agony of those open wounds at the moment. At least this way I can do what I need to without her trying to scratch my eyes out, or worse."

Rafe smiled, breaking some of the tension in the serious situation. "I thought you liked the worse?"

"Shut up and take my patient to the tub."

Rafe barely suppressed his laughter. He loved riling his friend up over his taste in women. Big, rough and often. That was Doc's motto.

He carried the cougar into his bathroom and eased her into the tub. "Jesus, Doc. The water is freezing."

He snorted. "It's not cold enough yet. You got any ice we can add?"

"Colder?" When Doc ignored him, Rafe took that as his answer. "Yeah, I can probably scrounge up something from the ice maker in the kitchen."

"Good. I need some supplies so I'll get it. You stay here and watch her." Doc stood.

"What exactly do you want me to do? I don't think she's going anywhere."

Doc sighed. "What in the world is up with you today? Just make sure she doesn't drown, okay?"

Rafe looked down at the woman in his tub. What was up with him? Ha! Loaded question. For one, seeing the woman naked despite her injuries made him very uncomfortable. The kind of uncomfortable that made him adjust his jeans discretely so he didn't embarrass himself. What kind of jackass gets turned on by a half dead woman turning blue in his tub? Fucking nut job, that's who.

He crouched beside the porcelain enclosure and touched her skin. Doc was right. She was literally burning up from the inside out. He grabbed a sponge from the nearby dish and began dripping cool water over her heated flesh. The ugly cuts on her arm and leg looked deep and terrifyingly dangerous. If she couldn't shift then they'd have to be stitched up to heal. If they got the poison taken care of.

Rafe squeezed water across her exposed stomach and could have sworn she twitched. His core tightened and his chest began to constrict. Even with the cuts, bruises and blood she was a beautiful woman. He couldn't imagine who wanted to do this to her or why. The females in his pack were treated like queens. If anyone ever laid a finger on one of them the consequences would be swift and fatal. Who would defend this woman? Did her pride not care?

*You do.* Goddamn wolf needed to shut up. Still, he continued to move the water across the feline's body. He didn't want her to die like this.

"I don't know who you are or why you've walked into my woods, but you're going to live. Do you hear me? Whatever is going on inside there, if you can hear me, then fight back. Do whatever it takes to just live. Let the animal do her job."

The more he talked to her, the angrier he grew. Someone had wanted her dead and he needed to know why. There were a lot of whys floating in and out of his head at the moment. Why her? Why now?

He laid the sponge down and gripped her hand. Long, strong fingers settled perfectly inside his. He stayed beside her and listened intently for a sign she was listening. Her heart beat steady, and her breathing had eased despite sounding shallow. Her body temperature had reduced at least a few degrees from what he could tell by touch.

He ached to pull her into his arms and hold her close. Whatever darkness had brought her to his doorstep they would fight together. That's what nature called for when she delivered your mate.

*Mate.*

He still wasn't ready to voice the word out loud. Although the way it slid through his mind felt more natural than he'd expected. After all the years of searching and wondering if someone out there was fated for him, she'd stumbled into his life on her deathbed. Not the aggressive she wolf he'd wished for though. Now, when tensions were higher than ever between the felines and the wolves, fate had delivered his mate. What a bitch fate could be. First, this one had to survive and he was helpless to save her. No! Doc would help her and she would recover. Of course, that left the matter with Tanner and the rest of his pack.

God help them all if they went against his mate.

# CHAPTER
# FOUR

Kitty struggled to wake up from the strange dream sucking her in. Where was all the growling and cursing coming from? She struggled to move and found her arms and legs too heavy to cooperate. Whatever the hell dream she'd gotten stuck in was quickly turning into a nightmare. The only exception was a man's voice, deep and caring, calling out to her. She opened her eyes to see him, at least she thought they were open but there was nothing but a sea of black in front of her.

*"C'mon, cat girl, you can do this."*

The voice came to her from what sounded like the far end of a tunnel. Normally someone calling her cat girl would have annoyed her, but for some reason the voice soothed her no matter what it said. If she could get out of this bed or whatever she was stuck to she'd investigate. Frustration clouded her thought processes. She just wanted to know what was going on. Her eyes started to burn and she steeled her emotions against them. *You will not fucking cry. Those feline bitches did this to you. No matter what happens, you will not cry. They do not deserve the satisfaction.*

Kitty pulled and thrashed in a desperate attempt to get some traction. After struggling for several minutes, she gave her body a break. Whatever mysterious shit she'd gotten into wasn't about to let her move. It would take her mind and will together to get her through this mess. She blew out a hard breath at that thought. She was sick and tired of being kicked down. Never in a million years would she have dreamed her life would come to this. She had nothing to show for her twenty-six years except shame, scandal and a wealth of hatred that festered inside her.

With everything she'd ever known stripped away from her, she no longer had purpose. It had been easy to follow her father's direction all her life while struggling to get her own way at every turn. She didn't care that her efforts backfired more often than they succeeded. That life had purpose, warped as it was.

For the first time in her life she wished for a new life, one that didn't include shifters and their self-righteous beliefs. It didn't matter that she'd been well on board with her ass backwards culture until recently. Something else had always called to her, something different. She just had to figure out what it was.

If she survived.

Dream or not, everything fucking hurt. As far as she could tell, every inch of her body had been damaged, inside and out. She had to escape the pain or go mad. Fortunately, or maybe unfortunately, a memory of her father drifted into her mind. As a cub she'd been no stranger to fights. The aggressive hormones that would later guide her direction were a major hurdle as a young girl. Every time someone annoyed her she simply wanted to scratch their eyes out. One particular summer, some of the other felines had begun stalking her. After weeks of being taunted, Kitty had grown tired of their games and decided to fight back. It hadn't been easy taking on the older girls, but it had been worth every ache and pain. Until she'd arrived home.

At the sight of her battered body, her father had gone into one of his many rages. She'd never doubted where her temper came from. She thought he would be proud she'd stood up for herself. Oh boy, had she been wrong. He'd dragged her by the hair through the entire clan until he'd made her apologize to each and every girl in front of a growing crowd.

"No daughter of mine will ever behave like common trash. You ever embarrass me like this again and I'll make you regret you were born." Those barbed words were hurled at her heart moments before he threw her inside a small cage barely big enough for her to turn around in.

"Since you feel the need to act like a common animal then I'll treat you like one." The click of the lock that had held her captive turned her stomach and caused a deep yowl to burst from her throat. Her father turned his sharp gaze on her and narrowed his eyes.

"Don't even think about retribution, little girl. The more you act out, the more I'll come down on you. I've got plenty of ways to make you suffer for each and every act of rebellion. Think about that tonight when you're cold and hungry and maybe tomorrow you'll have a different attitude." With his final hateful words, and the emotionless look in his eyes, her father turned away from her and climbed the stairs from the sound-proofed basement underneath their cabin. As darkness engulfed her, fear had crawled along her skin and tears burned behind her eyes. Somehow she'd held them in. The instinct to fight or flee that she struggled with on a daily basis had diminished in the days to follow.

Once a day her father had climbed down the stairs, shone a bright white light in her face and asked her the same question. "Are you ready to beg for forgiveness, little girl?" Each day when she refused to answer him, he called her an ungrateful bitch and walked away from her.

By day five, her body had ached, she was so hungry it felt like her stomach had turned inside out and she'd begun to hallucinate, some of her greatest fears coming to life in the dark. When the bastard didn't come down to ask his question that night she panicked. She'd tried to scream and hardly a squeak came out. Time slipped away and she had no idea if it was night or day. When the door finally opened she no longer trusted her ability to determine what was real and what wasn't.

Until her father appeared in the dim light and flashed the bright bulb in her face until it burned her retinas. The question came and Kitty no longer had the ability to answer. But she must have made some sort of sound because her father hauled her out of the cage and carried her back into their house. He never said another word about it and she had to stumble and fend for herself for food before she managed to fall into her bed and sleep for nearly twenty-four hours. It was two weeks before her father talked to her again, while choosing to pretend nothing out of the ordinary had happened between them.

She had never forgotten or truly forgiven. The gut wrenching pain and humiliation of being forced to admit she was no better than a backwater alley cat while she lay starving in a cage had burned inside her for years after that night. Admittedly, before the incident she'd been a handful. Trouble managed to find her no matter what she did or didn't do, but nothing had ever come from it beyond a handful of jealous felines who loved to goad her. The same feline bitches that tried to kill her...

But never again did she defy her father. He'd broken her and turned her into a tough, mean woman who looked out for herself, since no one else would. Until he'd kidnapped Malcolm's little girl.

*"Time to wake up and get your lazy bones out of my tub, pretty girl. You're going to hog all the water."*

The dark rumble of the stranger's voice began to pull her out of her memories of the past. She wanted to open her eyes and see his face again. Why was he talking to her? In her head she heard the cat inside begin to purr. The jolt of the animal's reaction coursed through her. Her blood warmed and the will to fight her way out this mess began to return. A vision of dark hair tumbling across a forehead above mesmerizing dark eyes beckoned her. Kitty grasped the instinct inside and put all her focus on seeing the man she knew kept vigil at her side.

S imon returned to the bathroom and Rafe moved out of the way so his friend could save her life. He stood close and watched while Doc packed some sort of funky goo into each dangerous looking cut before stapling the skin back together.

"Is that going to work? It fucking stinks." His lip curled as he spoke.

Simon shrugged. "I have no idea. The combination of herbs should break down the toxins but she'd have a hell of a lot better chance if she shifted. Ninety five percent of all injuries are naturally healed with the magic of a shift. Or at least it starts the healing process. This." He waved his hand across her body. "This is more like treating a fragile human. They can't heal like we do."

"Then why not give her some penicillin or some shit those human doctors think works so well? Isn't that scientist friend of yours working on something?" asked Rafe.

"Just because she looks human right now, we both know better. I'd need a damned barrel of penicillin for her body to use before it got metabolized out of her system."

Rafe held her hand while Doc continued to work. The fine porcelain skin of her arms and shoulders beckoned him. With little thought to anything other than his need to touch, he rubbed his thumb across her palm. He wasn't sure he believed the old wives tales that an animal's touch during times of distress had the power to soothe, but he'd try anything at this point.

The restless sleep of the woman in front of him kept his wolf on edge. When a small worry mark appeared on her forehead when she frowned, he took two fingers and drew them back and forth across the skin until her face once again relaxed.

He worried about the possible dreams that disturbed her rest. Without knowing the full details of her situation he'd have to be extra vigilant about her future safety.

Rafe shook his head. His thoughts were insane. He knew nothing about this woman other than what he saw and an imagined mystical connection wasn't going to cut it. He thought about peppering Simon with more of his questions and then decided against it. They had a little more time.

The silence stretched between him and Simon, but not uncomfortably so. They'd been close friends for decades and their companionship was but one of the many reasons he'd chosen the man as his second. The current pack Alpha was about to relinquish control and he'd already announced his decision to name Rafe as his successor. There was still the formality of a ceremony and there remained the possibility someone would challenge him for the position, not something Rafe had seriously considered until now.

"What's going on here, Rafe?"

Simon's question didn't surprise him. His infamous poker face that he managed to use at great success during his weekly games, didn't work all that well on his best friend. The fact he'd maintained physical contact with the injured shifter every second he was in the room also hadn't helped. That didn't mean he wanted to talk about it.

"Too soon to say. Guess we'll see if she lives first and then go from there," he answered.

"Go where exactly?" Simon pressed. "The hair on my neck stood at attention the moment you called and I don't think it's settled since. You have some sort of connection to this woman."

Rafe rubbed at his neck and forced himself to release her hand. The fact Simon hadn't phrased his statement as a question worried him. "I don't want to get into this now. We've got the pack change coming up, a new round of negotiations with the feline clan, and far too much trouble coming out of the neutral zone lately. I don't think we need to go borrowing problems just yet."

Simon waited for two solid minutes before he responded. "So you think getting involved with a female feline is going to help all that? If this is about sex..."

Rafe narrowed his eyes and snarled at his friend. "I think you know me better than that so don't be an asshole. I found her like this and I don't know a thing about her so, no this definitely is *not* about sex."

His friend turned to look at him, a serious expression across his face. "How exactly did she come to be in your possession, Rafe? I sense there's a lot you haven't told me yet. What the hell happened to her?"

Rafe stood and strode across the room and back. "You know as much as I do at this point. I found her with Tanner, He claimed he didn't do this to her and then almost challenged me when I took her from him. I made the decision to bring her here the minute I saw her crumpled and bleeding on the forest floor. He'd taken one look into the eyes of Tanner and his friends and known exactly what they planned to do to her next. We wolves may be a lot of things but it isn't necessary to be a savage among men all of the time. Plus another feline death isn't going to help our cause in a new peace negotiation."

A low whistle sounded behind his back. "He's probably already reported the finding. Have you called the Alpha?"

"No, I haven't called the Alpha. Jesus, I was a bit preoccupied with saving her life."

"Well, maybe you better start thinking about saving your ass before Burke comes knocking at your door demanding answers. Like who the hell is she and what is she doing on our land? She gave up her rights the minute she got here." Doc's voice grew low. "Oh and don't forget the part where you've bonded with her."

Rafe whipped around to face his friend. "What the hell did you just say?"

"You heard me. And don't even bother denying the connection. I can smell it all over you. I don't know what's going on in that pretty boy head of yours but this has got to be your worst fucking idea ever."

A rough growl erupted in Rafe's throat. Friend or no friend, the wolf didn't like his tone of voice. If Simon wanted to pick a fight with him, he was ready.

Simon held up his hands in mock surrender. "Don't take it out on me just because I'll stand up to you and say what needs to be said. This is a fuck up of major proportions and if she survives the night it's only going to get worse."

*If she survived*. His stomach dropped somewhere around his knees. "What are her chances?" She had to live. There was a lot about him he hadn't shared with Simon. Like the fact he'd grown restless and edgy the past six months. If Tanner wanted a dominance challenge, Rafe would welcome it.

Simon shrugged. "Hard to say."

"You know me, Simon. Give me a number, I need facts," Rafe pressed.

"I'd say fifty-fifty or less. Better if she shifts. Her fever's down some now so I think it's safe to move her back to the bedroom. Then, only time will tell."

Rafe didn't waste a second. He quickly lifted the woman from the tub and carried her back to the guest room. He glanced momentarily at the door to his own bedroom and shook it off. There was inappropriate and then there was *INAPPROPRIATE*.

With the swiftness of an unaffected friend, Rafe placed her on the cool sheets and took the offered towel from Doc to wipe the excess moisture from her skin. Instead of the satin smooth surface underneath his hands, Rafe's thoughts shot to Tanner and his little gang as they'd approached her in the forest. Fresh anger built inside him at the intent he'd spied on each of their faces. Ten minutes later and he would have been too late. She'd be dead or worse and the wolf inside him would have naturally sought vengeance.

"Careful, Rafe, I don't want you pulling those staples apart," Simon warned from the other side of the bed.

He glanced down at the white knuckled grip he had on her wrist. He really was losing it.

"Let me take her home with me. I can take care of her until she heals and then I can turn her over to the Alpha to decide her fate. This is way too dangerous for you."

Rafe shot the Doc a hard look. "No."

"You can't do this," said Simon.

Rafe stood and stared down the other wolf. He'd had enough. It was time Simon remembered his place. "I've always appreciated your input on my decisions but there's a line and you're crossing it. I've said no and I mean no. End of story. If you don't like it then I'll choose another."

His friend's face visibly paled but to his credit, he stood his ground. "Now wait just a minute. I'm only looking out for you here." Simon lifted his hand to cover the woman.

"Don't touch her," Rafe growled.

Simon jerked back a few steps, surprise obvious in his eyes. Rafe sighed and brushed his hands across his face. He understood how unreasonable he was being. If he was a smart man he'd let the Doc take her out of here and never see her again. Too bad that wasn't him.

"I don't think it's a good idea for you to touch her anymore." His skin crawled just having Simon this close to her.

"Don't you think that's taking things a bit overboard? Whether you see it or not, you're losing it, Rafe. For a feline."

"I'm not going to argue about this anymore. My decision is made. She is staying here and once she is well, I'll figure out what comes next. Until then the Alpha can cool his heels." He waited tensely for Simon to acknowledge his decision. When the slight dip of his head indicated his submission in the matter, Rafe relaxed a fraction. He hated pushing his friend to this point, but it wouldn't do for either one of them to forget who would ultimately be in charge.

When he took over as Alpha some things would stay the same, but many things would change forever.

For decades they'd seen very little change in pack policies and the world was closing in on them. It was time to grow and accept things can't stay the same forever. If he couldn't stop the rising war between the felines and the wolves, then it would be only a matter of time before the humans figured out what they really were. Dead bodies tended to draw lots of unwanted attention.

First, he still had the matter of whether or not she'd recover and Tanner's ridiculous claim over her.

"I'm going to stay here tonight, if you don't mind. There's no way to gauge how her body will respond to this treatment and I might have to take a whole new approach. I'll set up a bed on the couch." He picked up his bag and strode from the room without a backwards glance.

Rafe smiled. Simon always had his back even when he was pissed. He didn't enjoy exerting his will over his friend but there were times when showing control was necessary. They might look like humans most of the time, but they weren't. The wolf was never far from the surface and many of their actions were driven by animal instinct. Any sign of weakness from an alpha left the door open for another to come in and challenge him. Simon might not have been up for the challenge. but they'd fought over less in the past.

Rafe paced the floor to the opposite side of the room. He needed some distance between what had happened with Simon and the woman lying in his guest bed. He pulled back the curtains and stared into the dark. Twilight had turned to pitch-black hours ago and he hadn't even noticed. The moon shone near full from high above the tree line. They were getting close to the full moon and the pull of that washed over his skin. Another week and the leadership would change. Normally on a night like this he'd be out on a run, chasing rabbits and other game on a hunt with other pack. The sexual draw of the moon didn't help matters much either. He already had sex on the brain long before he'd stumbled into Tanner's little party in the woods.

Ever since the Alpha had allowed Tanner to join the pack there'd been trouble. He'd been injured in a hunting accident with several other shifters that had left him homeless and desperate. Never a good combination for a strong alpha male with an attitude problem. Instead of embracing the new pack, he'd spent the last six months fighting them. Even Burke, the Alpha, had seemed to grow weary of his belligerence. Unfortunately Tanner was an alpha himself, which made it especially difficult for him to submit to other's ways without a fight. Rafe seemed pretty certain the challenge from Tanner would be coming any day now. And now he was facing the very real possibility that a mate bond had begun to form with a feline. And not just any feline either. She'd been captured, possibly fair and square, and the bastard wouldn't simply stand by and let Rafe keep his new possession.

Acid burned in Rafe's stomach as he thought of Tanner or any of his hard ass buddies laying a hand on the woman in his bed. He'd see them all dead before it happened like that.

A soft rustle of sound drew his attention from the window and to the bed across the room. The pretty little shifter stirred under the mountain of blankets that Doc had left her under.

"What's going on? What happened?" Her voice was barely a whisper but Rafe heard her with no trouble. One of the many benefits of acute shifter senses.

He eased his body next to her on the mattress and she immediately recoiled in the opposite direction.

"Easy, little cat. I'm not planning to hurt you."

"Already hurt. Skin is on fire. What did you do to me?"

The biting sarcasm gave Rafe hope. If she had the energy to get feisty with him, then surely she had the fortitude to survive. Although the flushed color of her skin and sweat across her brow let him know she wasn't out of the woods yet. Her body still raged with fever. "Not me. I only found you like this. You don't remember anything?"

She turned her dark green gaze on him and he felt himself sinking into the warm depths. For a few seconds he held his breath while he watched her pink tongue poke from her mouth to lick her lips. "Hurts so much," she whispered.

"You need to shift," he insisted.

Her eyes grew wide with obvious alarm he didn't quite understand. "Can't."

"Sure you can. Don't worry about me, I've pretty much already figured out the truth."

Her small gasp confused him. He'd given her no reason to be alarmed. "You're safe here. I swear. You can shift and none from my pack will get past that threshold unless I allow it."

A breath later her nostrils flared and her eyes widened even further. He watched the recognition dawn across her features as she figured out her predicament.

"Wolf," she hissed. Despite the jagged cut across her left check she managed to scowl at him in a familiar amount of disgust. It wasn't easy for their clans to get along.

The air in the room shifted, pulling him from his thoughts and the pungent scent of fear filled the space around him. The impulse to react flooded through him as he fought to remain perfectly still. Her fear called to him. The wolf whined in his head. If she so much as moved he'd have to chase her and prove his dominance over her. The wolf would allow nothing less. Fortunately for them both, the harsh scent of her pain overrode the fear. Rafe shook his head to clear his confusion and focused on her emotions. She was in agony and the longer she laid there, the worse it got.

"Forget the wolf. I can handle him. Shift," he demanded.

"I can't," she cried.

A lone tear escaped the corner of her eye and tore at Rafe's senses. He didn't understand why she wouldn't shift and this feeling of helplessness made him feel like shit. "I promise. No one will hurt you. But if you don't shift soon you won't heal and then you'll end up dead in my house. So far beyond the treaty line none of your kind will come looking for you. Is that what you want? To die among us wolves?" His voice had a hard edge to it, more so than probably necessary, but he needed her to obey.

"Promises are nothing but lies."

Despite not knowing her at all, her response pissed him off. He'd offered her his protection and he wasn't accustomed to anyone not taking him for his word. A renewed flare of arousal rushing through his blood caught him off guard. The contradiction of the entire situation fueled the need for her trust. Her compliance became paramount. The wolf demanded it.

"I don't lie. You may not be in safe territory, but as long as you're in my house you *are* safe." He tried to speak softly but her pain affected him as well. Instead he snarled at her.

"Hate the fucking safe zone anyway," she choked. "I would rather die."

"Strong words from a woman now lying on her death bed."

"Fuck you. I didn't ask you to save me," she spat.

"Don't tempt me," he warned. She had a mouth on her that riled him to no end. Unbidden images flooded his mind with a multitude of things she could do with such a filthy mouth. He growled, probably more at himself than her, but she didn't know that.

Anger rolled from them in thick waves, filling the room with tension. Along with it, Rafe added some shift magic, allowing some of his features to change and elongate. Hair grew on his face. His teeth lengthened. By God she would obey him.

The woman in front of him didn't cower in fear. Instead she bared her teeth and hissed.

*Mate.* His inner wolf thought it again.

No. Unacceptable. He refused to believe what the wolf insisted on. He waited and hoped. If only she backed away or made a move...

Rafe lifted his head and howled. The sound rattled the furniture in the room as well as the windows. Frustration coiled inside him and then she moved. Her magic reached out and brushed him. He jumped to his feet and curled his lips at the golden colored cougar now residing in his bed. The woman had disappeared and the cat had taken over. He should have been offended at the sight of her but instead his erection grew. Rafe started forward until a hand on his shoulder stopped him.

"Don't."

His friend had returned and now tried to stop the wolf from taking what he thought belonged to him. Fuck that. He shook from the man's hold, prepared to fight anyone who tried to stop him.

"Look at her," Simon whispered. "She can't take you on."

Rafe forced himself to stand still and examine the gorgeous feline. Light tawny hair covered a compact solid body. His gaze froze on one of the gashes still oozing dark blood. Her chest fell and rose in rapid succession, as if she was struggling to catch her breath. With her distress more than evident, Rafe's wolf began to settle, albeit with a whine of protest.

"She didn't heal."

Simon moved beside Rafe but apparently knew better than to get too close to the feline just yet. Not only did he have to worry about her fighting him, but Rafe's wolf was still on edge and wouldn't tolerate another man touching her in his heightened state of agitation.

"No, not completely. Some of the minor scrapes and cuts look better but the poison did a number on her."

Rafe turned to his friend. "Will she recover?"

Simon nodded and lowered his voice to barely audible. "She's not going to die but I'm afraid she's not going to be the same." He nodded his head to the door and indicated for Rafe to follow him.

He turned back to the woman. Her ears were pinned back to the top of her head and he swore he read pain and distrust in her gaze. Not that he had to rely on his intuition or sight. Her scent told him all he needed to know. She carried so much anger, but it simply masked the pain she clung to. Whatever her story was, it was certainly more than he'd seen thus far.

He shut his eyes tight and forced the wolf to back down. The muscle in his jaw twitched as he regained control and his features returned to human. He'd have time later to press her for details. For now she needed to rest and he needed answers from Simon.

## CHAPTER
# SIX

K itty watched the wolf disappear through the door and chuffed out a hard breath. She held her defensive position for a few seconds longer before she collapsed onto the bed, shifting back to human. The strain to hold her feline form had consumed the last of her energy reserves.

The doctor had tried to lower his voice on her verdict, but they'd known no matter how low he spoke she would overhear every word with her supernatural hearing. Kitty rolled to her uninjured side and sought a comfortable position, an impossible feat. Thanks to her shift, the fire burning inside her wounds had dulled to a steady simmer. Of course, she wasn't about to admit that her shift had been a direct result of the alpha wolf demanding her submission. Asshole.

The magic of the feline, however, never ceased to amaze her, even if her ability was the complete opposite of everyone else she knew. Still, the troubling observation that her body wasn't healing as easily as it should weighed heavily on her mind.

It wouldn't take much to listen in on what the two men in the other had to say about her condition, but she tuned out the noise and rested her head on her hand. She already knew these were no ordinary wounds and while they might heal, they would leave her irreparably damaged.

Fucking feline bitches.

Anger pumped through Kitty's blood as she relived the scene outside the supposed safe house over and over. They'd lain in wait for her and probably would have killed her had she not managed to break loose. What troubled her even more was the uncertainty of whether or not the attack had been clan sanctioned. Just because the guardian had offered her a reprieve didn't guarantee the council would accept his recommendation as the last word. Most of the clan believed the public hearings were final and that all council decisions were made public. Little did they know her father had pulled their strings so many times and usually got whatever he wanted.

While her father had declared her useless and largely ignored her presence, Kitty had spent much of her time listening and observing everything that went on around her. Like her father, many of the council elders liked to take matters into their own hands and in private. Their decisions were often brutal and archaic, not to mention secret.

Unfortunately her escape from the felines had not gone as well as she'd hoped. Landing in the middle of wolf territory had left her well and truly screwed. Her memories of what happened after that still remained rather fuzzy but she did remember the three male shifters who'd nearly attacked her. Unfortunately, how she'd ended up here in *his* house eluded her.

Rafe. She heard the doctor saying his name. The image of his ruggedly handsome face floated through her memory where it had been imprinted the first time she'd seen him. Kitty struggled to recall all of the details. Somehow she'd ended up in his arms and he'd carried her here. That much she knew for certain. But there was something else about him... Something in her brain she felt she should remember. The knowledge burned into her as steadily as the poison.

Determined to discover more about him, she glanced around the room. The small bedroom, while sparsely decorated, had a light and airy feel to it. From the cream colored walls to the light oak hardwood floors, she got the impression the space was designed to make a guest feel relaxed and comfortable. There wasn't much more than the double bed she laid on, a small dresser across the room and a nightstand next to her. There was a door next to the dresser that she assumed led to a closet. In the far corner stood a gorgeous full-length mirror, antique from what she could tell. Her gaze admired every curve and carving in the wood surrounding it. She would love to have such a pretty piece in her home. A moment later, reality intruded and she remembered all too clearly that she no longer had a home. Even the shitty safe house Kane had offered her had slipped through her grasp.

No home, nowhere to run. The desolation engulfed her.

Despite the feeling of being trapped, Kitty's instincts forced her to think about this room. She ached to prowl through the space and search for clues about what she'd gotten herself into, but the energy to move had escaped her. So instead, she closed her eyes and concentrated on the healing magic she needed so desperately. The familiar tingle washed over her without causing the change. She'd discovered as a teenager that she could manipulate the power in small degrees without taking it all the way to a shift. This allowed her to heal wounds, move faster in her human form and enhanced her senses equal to the cat. Something no one else in her pride could manage, that she knew of. Another anomaly she'd yet to solve.

The power sizzled at the site of her wounds and a yowl of protest filled her head. Sweat beaded on her forehead and her limbs began to tremble.

"What are you doing?"

Kitty jerked at the voice right next to the bed. She hissed in response.

He'd snuck up on her without a sound. Goosebumps rose along her arms and her fingers curled defensively. The nagging sensation she got every time he got close plagued her mind. She shrugged it off as a side effect of her weakened condition. Obviously the poison had multiple affects she wasn't aware of.

"No need to be pissy. I'm only trying to help you."

Despite Rafe's words, and her diminished strength, her muscles coiled rigidly and her fingers curled, ready for claws. "Don't want your help," she murmured.

"Oh, okay then. Does that mean you'd like me to deliver you back into the woods so those idiots I found you with can finish what they started?"

Heat pumped through her. The urge to knock the smirk from his face rode her hard. Unfortunately she didn't possess the control to shut her own mouth, let alone his. "Is that why you brought me here? So you could taunt me? I mean, what's the point of bringing me here if you only want to send me back? Or were you hoping to fuck me first, because I'm not about to become someone's fuck toy. So go ahead and get that shit out of your pretty little head right now." She didn't bother to hide the distaste from her voice. He was a damned wolf and likely to kill her or worse once she healed. It was the worse that gave her pause. It didn't take much imagination at all to know what the other men from the woods would do to her. It was this one who confused her. She couldn't get a bead on his motives yet and that fact exhausted her.

Then there was her body's reaction...

Rafe pulled the chair she'd failed to notice close to the bed and sat down, bringing him closer in view. Dark hair framed a unique face with angular planes. Even darker eyes stared down at her, mesmerizing her. They reminded her of melted chocolate on a hot sunny day. She loved chocolate.

"I brought you here because you were a bloody, beat up mess and I didn't like the look in Tanner's eyes when he stared down at you."

His direct and seemingly honest answer threw her off guard and her expression softened for a split second before the suspicions grew stronger. "That's a nice story. But you're wolf and I'm not. I don't believe for a second you want to help me. You hate our kind."

He sat back and sighed, his gaze never wavering from her face. "I don't blame you for not trusting me, but you're going to have to find a way past that if you want to come up with a solution. I don't hate a whole species unilaterally. My decision to like or not like someone is based on the individual."

"But you're—"

He held up his hand and stopped her protest. "Yeah, yeah, I know. Feline and wolves are enemies and have been for decades. Don't you ever get tired of hearing that? Saying it? Living it?" he pushed his fingers through his hair. "We have a lot in common, you know."

Kitty scoffed. She couldn't imagine a single thing she'd have in common with his kind.

"No, seriously. We may not share the same animal DNA, but we do have our human traits in common. We eat, sleep, go to work and socialize the same. Who's to say we can't find more."

"You're even crazier than I thought," she whispered. "Are you going to break out in song and sing about how we should all just get along? Cause if so, I'm getting the hell out of here before you do." She started to struggle into a sitting position and failed.

The wolf growled, a dark shadow crossing his face. That single look made her stomach quiver and her pulse ratchet up a notch or two. As usual she'd let her mouth get the best of her and she'd pissed off the lone man who now held her life in his hands.

*Smooth move, Kitty.*

"I bet that smart mouth gets you into a lot of trouble. It at least gives me some insight into your current condition. What happened? Did you push someone too far and get into a fight?"

Kitty recoiled at his assessment. Renewed anger sparked through her, setting off the fire in her wounds to an even higher level. The gasp of pain slipped from her lips before she could stop it.

Rafe jumped to his feet. "What happened? Is it worse?"

When she didn't immediately respond, he leaned forward into her personal space. "Tell me."

"Hurts," she managed through gritted teeth.

"I should get Doc. You need something for the pain."

Without thought she reached for his arm and stopped him before he could spin and walk out the door. "Not yet. I just need some time to get myself straight." Kitty watched his brows draw together as he considered which route to take. After what felt like forever, he finally backed off and assumed the seat next to her bed.

While her mind still demanded answers, her body was again at the point of no return. She wanted nothing more than to roll over and sleep for a week.

"Why don't we start over with something easy. My name's Rafe. What's yours?" He held out his hand and waited for her to take it.

Her right arm didn't hurt as much as her left so she grasped his palm and answered, "Kitty."

A wide smile transformed his face and took her breath away. He went from dark and devilish to boyishly handsome in a matter of seconds. "Seriously?"

Kitty rolled her eyes and lifted her head to stare at the ceiling. "Yes, seriously." As if she hadn't heard that sarcasm before. A feline named Kitty. Ha. Ha. Ha.

"Is Kitty short for something else?"

Her breath clogged in her throat. The way her name rolled from his tongue sent a slight tremor down the length of her spine. How he'd managed to make such a simple question sound so sensuous was beyond her comprehension. Not to mention the slight crack in her self-preservation his voice created. For a moment she wanted to think they were friends. That her visit here was both temporary and voluntary and when she healed she'd simply get up and walk out.

Fat chance. She admonished her thoughts.

"Nope. Just Kitty." As far as she was concerned, the woman her father called Katherine was long gone.

"Okay, just Kitty. Do you remember why or how you wandered from clan land onto wolf territory?"

Kitty strained to remember the events of the day before. The council had banished her from her home and magically branded her as an outcast, effectively leaving her nowhere to go except the neutral zone. This wasn't exactly the kind of information she wanted to pass on to her captor. If she held nothing useful for him there would be no reason for him to keep her alive. She needed to think fast. Sooner or later he'd notice the brand and then he'd know the truth.

"Let's just say I pissed off some women in the clan and yesterday they decided to get back at me."

He quirked his right brow. "I'd say they were pretty angry to bring poison to a fight. What exactly did you do?"

Panic quivered through her. She wasn't about to give her life story to this... this... stranger.

Another small smile crept over his face. "Don't want to tell me all your secrets, huh?"

Kitty kept her mouth closed for once.

"Fine, although you might be surprised by how much I already know. If my memory serves me there is a feline named Kitty from your clan who is the daughter of former council member Bran, who happens to be the one who died recently after causing a shitload of trouble for your guardians. Am I right?"

In fact, I believe he was obsessed with their power and for years went back and forth between revenge and some pretty crazy experiments. That's how you ended up with a hybrid half sister isn't it?

Her insides froze and her stomach roiled, threatening to revolt. How in the hell did he know private clan business? Was there a wolf spy in their midst?

Rafe sat back in his chair and weaved his fingers over his chest. "I like that wild eyed look you get when I surprise you." He suddenly leaned forward and brought his face perilously close to hers. "I'm right, aren't I? I know all about the Guardian trouble going on between the felines and you've been right in the middle of it thanks to your father. All kinds of people gossip, both wolf and feline."

Kitty could only whimper her distress as all the vile things she'd done came rushing forward. The more she thought over what brought her here the more she realized the apple did not fall far from the tree. Blood was thicker than water and she truly was Bran's daughter.

"I'm not here to judge you, nor do I really care to know all the sordid details. What I am looking for is something I can use when Tanner takes his case to the pack." Rafe's breath caressed her heated skin. The scent of pine and man came on so strong it overtook her senses.

A new warmth crept through her. She no longer cared about the past. Instead, she focused on the fact every word out of his mouth seemed to make her tingle from head to toe.

"Tanner?" With all the cohesive thoughts abandoning ship, she couldn't remember who anyone was except the man in front of her.

At least until her head kicked in and she reminded herself what she faced. A very large, very dangerous wolf who'd plucked her from the brink of death for no good reason. Before she could respond, his beefy hand touched the side of her face. A spark sizzled along her skin and made her recoil from the connection.

"Don't worry. I'm just checking for fever." A slight smile followed his words and she noticed the transformation of his face instantly. He managed to go from big scary wolf to a man who gave her thoughts she definitely wasn't supposed to be having. The big, sweaty, sexy kind. As if on cue her breasts tingled and her stomach tightened.

"Your eyes changed color. Why is that?" He voiced the question on a heavy sigh, eliciting another buzz of reaction from her.

"Don't know," she lied.

For a few long seconds he stared at her as if he saw straight through her. The vulnerability that look created threatened to overwhelm her. She wanted to blink or look away but found it impossible to break eye contact. For a moment she forgot about the pain, the differences of their species and the fact she needed to get away. She focused only on the foreign sensation of being mesmerized. Her head and body betrayed her with a sharp longing for more of the man sitting in front of her who'd awakened something inside her with a simple touch to her cheek.

Did fate send her here to find her mate? Why would her mate be a wolf who'd rather kill her than keep her?

Before the question sank into the logical part of her brain a sudden prick of pain erupted in the fleshy part of her upper arm. She jerked from Rafe's touch and bared her teeth on a vicious hiss.

"What did you do?" Already the edges of her vision were beginning to blacken and she knew it was only a matter of seconds before she would be gone.

The wolf in front of her held up a small syringe. "It's for the best..."

Whatever else he'd said faded in her memory faster than her brain could process as she fell limp to the mattress and closed her eyes.

*Betrayed again.* It was her last thought before she succumbed to the darkness.

# CHAPTER
# SEVEN

"Is she awake?"

"No. It's going to be a while before she's conscious again. Thank God."

Kitty heard the voices but again couldn't see who was speaking. She desperately wanted to open her eyes but no matter how hard she tried they wouldn't cooperate. Both male voices were so familiar but her brain couldn't or wouldn't identify either one.

"Her wounds are finally starting to heal."

"I take it the last of the poison is gone now?"

*Poison? What poison? What was wrong with her? Why couldn't she wake up?*

"Looks like it, but she's not healing like she should. See this? This is serious scar tissue beginning to form."

"You mean all of these injuries are going to stay like that?" Whoever belonged to that dark silky voice needed to keep talking.

"I'm afraid so. Such a shame to see such a beautiful woman marred like that. She must have some serious enemies."

*Who the hell was he talking about?* Frustration beat at her skull as she struggled to comprehend what she'd overhead.

"She'll be healthy?"

"As healthy as you or I."

"But will she shift?"

The bed jostled around her. "I don't see why not. She's already shifted several times and lucky for her that seemed to work on the internals. It's just the skin where the poison lingered too long that's going to be a problem. I do need to change the bandages though."

"Go on home, Doc. I can do this."

"You sure? If she wakes up you're likely to have a hellcat on your hands. I have a feeling she isn't going to like the fact you shot her full of enough sedative to knock her out for days without telling her."

"I'll live. It won't be the first time I've managed to piss off a woman."

The second man laughed. "Rafe, when do you not have a woman ticked off at you? I've never seen any male so capable of riling up a woman's anger more than you."

Kitty tried to listen to the rest of the conversation between the two men but their voices faded and she still couldn't move. Whatever the bastard had given her did more than knock her out. The drug paralyzed her.

Pretty soon even the faint sound of their voices disappeared and the quiet engulfed her. Silence wasn't her thing. It unnerved her. In Kitty's life total quiet had always been a precursor to something very bad so she always made sure there was something going on. She kept to crowded places or used radio or television noise to fill the background, whatever it took to keep the silence at bay. Silence in her world equated to the cage in the basement.

With her mind on the verge of a break down, the bed shifted around her and a hand brushed against her. The pressure of the bandage on her arm lessened, evoking a whimper of distress from her.

"Is the pretty kitty awake?"

She could hear the mocking smile in the tone of his voice but she couldn't answer. When he was obviously satisfied she still slept, he went back to work on her bandages. For a few moments her head ached and she fought to open her eyes. While her attempts were futile, the strangest thing happened. The man next to her began to hum. An old country rock tune, if she wasn't mistaken.

One by one he worked on all of her bandages, only moving her when he had to it seemed. All the while he hummed that damn song and even sang a few lyrics now and then. The animal inside her yowled in appreciation and relaxed one muscle at a time. The pain had faded to a minor irritation and her body had grown heavy with a need for sleep. Now her secondary half tugged at her consciousness, pulling her down. It always amazed her when the DNA inside her shifted and she made out her distinct halves. One human, the other cougar. What in the world would a cougar do with a wolf?

Kitty smiled to herself. She'd have to think about that later. After she killed him for drugging her. Some of what happened to her was coming back. With the sound of Rafe's voice in her ear and the cat purring in her head she had no other choice but to succumb to the lull the sounds created. Without warning a warm finger traced from her eyebrow to her mouth. Little tingles of sensation electrified her skin from her head to her toes. Not to mention the warmth growing low in her belly. His deft touch disarmed her of some of the anger she harbored on a regular basis. Instead, her mind began to calm and she reveled in this strange man's touch. For a wolf he didn't act at all like she'd expected.

Of course, a little sympathy for an injured woman meant little in the light of day once she healed. There were consequences to everything...

Once whatever he gave her wore off enough for her to wake up, she'd come up with a plan to get free. She'd never gone down without a fight before and she wasn't about to start here. For now, the wolf's den would have to do. God help him when she got her strength back and remembered this shit. Whatever he gave her made her a sappy weak kitten with no backbone.

The cat yowled.

*Yeah, yeah. You like him. Whatever.*

The scene around Kitty dimmed as the fatigue wrestled control.

*Don't get used to this because there's no way in hell we are keeping him...*

# EIGHT

Rafe wandered from room to room with no clear direction. Kitty had slept through the night and the entire next day with no more than a few whimpers and some tossing and turning. In that time her wounds had healed enough for him to remove the gauze they'd been wrapped in. The severe scarring had not improved and that worried him.

First, he had no idea how she'd react and second if Tanner ever reclaimed her it would not go well. A more vain wolf he'd never met and he wouldn't take kindly to finding out what he'd hoped would be his new toy, was now disfigured.

Drawn to the sleeping form on the bed, Rafe stepped close to examine the puckered skin on her face. The angry red streaks of a fresh wound were still visible around the edges, but the skin had closed and it was easy to see what the results of her injury would now be.

As if she sensed his closeness, she twitched and turned in his direction. He held his breath and waited for her eyes to open. It had been too long since he'd last seen those eyes staring into his with a mixture of fear and defiance. When moments passed with no more movement, he exhaled. Despite the injuries, he'd barely been able to take his eyes off of her. In sleep she appeared peaceful, almost content. A far cry from the smart mouthed woman he'd bantered with.

Rafe smiled. Not that he minded that woman either. Her feistiness drew him to her as much as the animal instinct did. Long inky lashes fanned below her eyes, inviting him to observe more. The small, pert nose that fit her profile perfectly, to the lush lips that whispered words he couldn't make out the more she slept. Her lush mouth kept giving him fantasies that were wholly inappropriate. Not that the idea of being politically incorrect ever stopped him before.

Rafe tore his gaze from the soft pink skin of her lips and continued his perusal. The stubborn chin she kept raised in the air and the graceful column of her neck led to the best set of... Fuck. He had to stop thinking like that. Doc had allowed him to help bath and bandage her in a purely professional manner in the midst of a medical situation. And God knows he'd tried to keep his thoughts pure and his eyes off things he wasn't meant to see. Rafe blew out a hard breath and scrubbed his chin. He'd taken care to dress her in one of his long sleeve t-shirts so she'd be more comfortable. Uh huh. The more skin he kept covered the less likely anything inappropriate would occur between them. Who was he kidding? Fabric or no fabric the image of her tanned and silken skin had been burned into his brain and it wasn't going away. On the contrary, it had taken up residence and burrowed so deep into his psyche he saw naked flesh when there was none. And his dick had betrayed him as well by staying hard all day long. It served as an uncomfortable and constant reminder of everything he wasn't supposed to be thinking of.

Talk about ridiculous.

"What did you do to me?"

Rafe spun at the hoarse words behind him. Not only had the feline finally woken, but she struggled into a sitting position. He stared at her dumbfounded. Her blonde hair tumbled around her face and shoulders, reminding him of a woman fresh out of bed after a long night of sex.

Her legs peeked from underneath the blanket and his mouth went dry at the sight of smooth, tanned flesh that seemed to go on and on.

"My eyes are up here, asshole."

Rafe's head jerked up and met her gaze. She was not smiling. "I'm sorry. You just caught me off guard. I thought you'd sleep longer."

Kitty shrugged. "Kind of like you tricking me last night? If it was last night and not something crazy like last week. What the hell was that anyway? I had some seriously funky dreams."

"It was just a sedative Doc wanted you to have. You needed to heal and sleep was apparently the best way to accomplish it. It wasn't personal. Besides, you were fighting everything. Seems being here in my house does not make you comfortable at all."

Her head shot up. "Does that surprise you?" She waved her hands around the room. "I'm in your house. A wolf's house. Wherever the hell that is. And somewhere out there is a pack of feline bitches that apparently want me dead and a few more wolves who now think I'm their property. Did I remember everything correctly?"

"So you did listen to what we were saying? I wondered. I wasn't getting much of a reaction no matter what I said."

"Drugs'll do that to a person, you know. What do you want from me? Why did you bring me here and what do you care whether I heal or not? I'm nothing to you."

The anger in her words had begun to build until he felt the venom underlying each and every one. She assumed she meant nothing and under other circumstances she'd have been right. Felines from his experience were nothing but trouble. Over the decades they'd proven to be crafty and devious adversaries. The treaty his Alpha had negotiated might have kept the war at bay for now, but that didn't mean old hatreds and fears hadn't continued to simmer just below the surface for far too long.

"Don't assume to know my mind, little cat." He stepped closer. "I may be known for my patience but I'm equally known for my enough is enough attitude. And your pretty little mouth pushes you close to the latter category.

Kitty yanked up her sleeve and presented her mangled arm to him. "What are you planning to do that hasn't already been done? I've been cast out, beaten, poisoned and left for dead. Give it your best shot, Romeo, but don't fuck it up. I don't have the patience."

Rafe froze mid tirade. Outcast? He grabbed her right hand, turned it upside down and pushed up the sleeve. Sure enough, at the spot where her hand met her wrist the small witches symbol of an outcast had been etched into her skin.

How in the hell had he not noticed she'd been spelled as an outcast? What the fuck was the matter with him? His dick didn't have that much control. He dropped her hand and strode across the room. Just what he needed. One more strike against what his animal DNA insisted on. *Mate.*

Fuck that.

*Mate.*

The word wouldn't stay out of his head and the wolf inside would damn sure reinforce it. A fresh rush of outrage and anger boiled through his veins. A smart man would have left her in the clearing for Tanner to deal with. Let him deal with the penalty for keeping someone who'd been sentenced to the neutral zone. The one trump to trespassing law.

He whirled back to face her. "What did you do to get that?" he spat.

"Don't worry your pretty little head about it. All you have to do is let me go and forget all about it," Kitty snapped back.

Rafe snarled and moved close. "You'd like that, wouldn't you? Just let you wander off into the woods and back to what?" He grabbed her by the shoulders and hauled her against his frame. "Back to Tanner and his friends or maybe to your feline friends? Aren't they the ones who did this to you?"

Her eyes went wide and her mouth formed the perfect O. For a few delicious seconds he'd rendered her speechless and it was heaven. Her body aligned against his, her belly pressed against his rigid erection over which he apparently had no control. Her body heat seeping into his skin seemed to entice him further. Not to mention her scent. He got a nose full before she reared her head back and struggled from his grasp.

"Are you insane?" She fought against him wildly and he fully understood why they were often referred to as wild cats. It was a beautiful sight to behold.

"No, not quite insane but pretty close. I've been trapped in this house for days with unanswered questions and a need for something more." He kept his tone even but he banded his arm around her shoulders and grasped her firmly against his bodyweight. He wasn't worried she'd reinjure herself but he didn't want to take any chances. "Stop fighting," he commanded.

She ignored his request and instead redoubled her efforts. His grip faltered before he whipped her around and pressed her back to his front. The little hellcat froze. She must have felt what all her struggling was doing to him. During her struggle her shirt had ridden above her hips and his cock had wedged between her soft buttocks. Rafe struggled for a semblance of control while Kitty breathed hard in his arms. Her mussed hair had shifted and her now bare neck called to him stronger than any siren song. This was pure animal instinct.

Wolves took a bare neck as a strong sign of submission and he couldn't resist this one. He bent forward and gently grasped the tight tendon that ran along the top of her shoulders and neck between his teeth.

Kitty jerked, the sharp scent of fear radiating from her skin. "Rafe. What are you doing?"

His name fell from her lips for the first time and it took all he had and all he was as the next in line Alpha not to devour her on the spot. He had responsibilities to keep and an image to project. Yet he still sank his teeth a fraction into her flesh without piercing her skin and did the unthinkable. He lapped at her fragrant skin for the taste he couldn't resist.

Musk and honey flavored his tongue for a brief moment before he closed his mouth around her flesh and sucked. While he had enough control not to mark her with his bite, he needed to mark her somehow nevertheless. This was enough for now to offer a visible sign and a reminder to her who she really belonged to. Eventually she had to learn he wasn't letting her go.

She sagged against him and he tightened his hold to keep her from falling. Several pulls later he released her neck with a pop and buried his nose in her hair a fraction from her ear.

"Say it again?"

"What?" she whimpered.

"My name."

"No."

"Say it," he commanded.

"Rafe," she whispered.

His gut clenched at the breathless word. He had a feeling no matter how many times she said his name, it would never be enough.

"I need to touch you."

"You are touching me." Despite her attempt at sarcasm, he heard the slight tremble in her voice and the nearly invisible shake of her limbs. His stomach tumbled at her reaction, forever etching this woman in his mind.

"Bend over."

"Rafe." This time the word came out like a small plea. She might have meant it as a no, but he wasn't about to assume such a thing. There was no way either of them could deny the connection sizzling between them. Sexually, they would be matched.

He placed his palm at her shoulder and slowly slid down to the middle of her back. The heat of her skin through the flimsy shirt she wore only encouraged him to keep going. At the edge of the hem he hesitated until he caught the telltale tremble that told him just how affected she'd become.

The wolf roared forward and wrestled him for control. Rafe fought him back. This was no time to let things spiral completely out of control. Still, the animal instincts rode close to the surface as he dipped his fingers to the naked flesh beyond the shirt.

He closed his eyes and held his breath. Dear God. The simple touch of silky skin under his hand nearly drove him to his knees.

Kitty whimpered and wriggled a few inches.

"Shhh. Hold still or the wolf will go insane," he pleaded.

Fortunately she listened to him for once and stilled.

His skin itched and his body ached with need outside his comprehension. He was beyond playing with fire at this point. Still, his fingers caressed her backside as gently as possible. The alarm bells in his brain tried to warn him to stop before it was too late but he found her impossible to let go.

A sudden shudder swept through Kitty and Rafe dug his fingers into her backside to steady both the wolf and the woman. He easily stood at the edge of a cliff and one false move from either of them and they'd plunge headfirst into a shitstorm of trouble. When he was satisfied he could go easy he slid another few inches along the satin smooth expanse of her right buttock. He'd pretty much seen everything there was to see when she'd been injured but it didn't stop the craving to spread her wide so he could look to his heart's content.

His original concern for her grave wounds had managed to outweigh his desire, which kept him in line. Now the only thing holding him back was a thin imaginary line that neither he nor the wolf could afford to cross. A growl rumbled deep in his chest—a simple warning from the wolf that he wouldn't tolerate the shackles for long.

When his fingers reached the apex at the top of her thighs he didn't stop to question or coax. He simply slid between her lush legs and into the pool of moisture that awaited. The rumble turned to a whine as his vision blurred around the edges and the colors of the room blinded him with contrast.

So wet.

"Jesus, Kitty."

With those two words her silence ended. Her whimpers fell one right after the other as she gyrated against his hand. "Can't. Not right. Oh God," she cried, all while her body sought more from him.

With her open and ready for him, Rafe nearly lost it.

*Have to stop. Have to stop.*

He chanted the words in his head over and over until his brain reengaged and he dropped his hand. They were both under the influence of instincts that could easily rob them of their senses. But the last thing he could tolerate right now would be for her to regret this when common sense prevailed once again. And it would, just as soon as he came inside the tight sheath he knew waited for him.

Mating frenzy was nature's way of ensuring the continuation of their race. Although nature obviously didn't discriminate between species like their human halves did. Something he'd do well to remember in situations like this. A child born between them would be branded as a half-breed and shunned from all but the most lenient packs. And Rafe's alpha was not known for his leniency.

The shock of his thoughts had the effect of cold water thrown in his face. Reality set in and he pushed Kitty's shirt down and lifted her torso to a standing position.

"You're right, we can't." He waited for the words to sink in for both of them while he held her close, her back to his front. The tight fit of his jeans from the hard-on had not eased and likely wouldn't do so for some time to come.

Kitty began to shake, first a little, and then violently in his arms. He desperately wanted to turn her and see the look in her eyes but he knew he couldn't. His resolve would not stand up against desire or pain shining back at him.

"There are more clothes in the drawers. Several of my nosy pack members have stopped by in the hopes of getting some salacious gossip about what we're doing in here. I figured the least some of them could do was bring you some clothing that might fit when you needed it. Please pick something out and stay completely covered. I don't think I need to explain what's going on here, do I?"

She slowly shook her head with nary a whimper despite the shakes quaking through her body. He hated to think about the vile things likely running in her mind at the moment. Whether she cursed him for stopping or starting in the first place didn't really matter. Nothing she said could be harsher than his own admonitions.

He fought the urge to fall into bed with her and simply hold her. He wanted to whisper assurances in her ear that all would be well. He doubted the realization of her true predicament had set in yet. Not her injuries, the scars and not even the trouble with Tanner. Speaking of... He needed to start working the pack before the Alpha called him in.

Reluctantly he released her and took a step back. She didn't turn or make any other movements other than to pull the shirt below the curve of her pretty little ass.

"Get dressed. We're going to have company." With that, he turned and walked from the room. Outside the door he stopped and leaned against the wall. His gut twisted and pain ripped through him.

*Mate. Mate. Mate.*

His brain might be engaged but his body clamored for the woman on the other side of the wall and apparently no amount of common sense was going to change that.

The minute Rafe left the room Kitty clutched her stomach and dropped to her knees. Her womb cramped and her heart raced wildly out of control. He'd had his hands all over her and at the time she would have gotten down on the floor and begged him to take her if he'd given her half a chance.

Heat flooded her face and neck. The embarrassment over her predicament floored her. Hadn't she learned her lesson last time? When Kane was her sole focus she'd been determined to do anything to ensure he mated her. That had definitely not gone well for her.

She'd learned a hard lesson that begging a man for his love and affection was what weak women did and she refused to be that woman anymore. When it came to her currently non-existent or future love life, she had no more tricks up her sleeves or any devious plans to get what she wanted.

Instead she suddenly wanted a wolf and that mortified her.

Somehow, his touch had branded her. She slid her hand down her backside and felt for the small indelible marks his fingers had left on her skin. She'd likely bruise later and for some reason that made her equally sad and happy. There was also the low throb at her neck where he'd held her with his mouth. He'd marked her in multiple ways and then suddenly came to his senses. How he walked away, she'd never understand. If it had been up to her they'd be screwing right now. Her sex squeezed, aching to be filled. His erection had pressed hot and heavy into her backside and she'd been embarrassingly ready. His fingers had easily found the proof of her desire, leaving her no option to deny what she felt.

Not that she was exactly a stranger to arousal. She enjoyed a pretty face and a warm body when she needed it. But this had been different. Intense. Intimate. Never in her life had she been so—so consumed. Good God, the man was going to kill her with need.

*Enough.*

She almost yelled the word across the room before she remembered he hadn't gone far. Any noise she made he would certainly hear. Sometimes the benefit of being a shifter became a curse. A benefit when it suited her, a curse when it betrayed her to the enemy. With some effort she stood and crossed the room to the dresser. She didn't want to consider Rafe the enemy no matter what her head said. The cougar had embraced the man, despite the wolf. Or maybe it was the wolf that called to her. That made no sense. But in his arms there had only been him and she wanted it all.

Kitty sighed. No matter, the whole thing was beyond fucked up. If she didn't leave soon... No, the consequences were too insane to ponder.

With a hard yank, she pulled open a drawer and rifled through the contents. All men's clothing that was far too large for her. She tried another drawer and found a stash of frilly panties and bras.

*Seriously?* Was this his idea of a joke or had some meddling wolf done this? Kitty dug deeper and finally emerged with a pair of camouflage pants and held them up. They were not her size, but at least they had a drawstring she could use to pull them tight around her waist. They'd have to do.

She also grabbed a black tank top and the least frilly bra should could find. Satisfied enough with her choices, she padded into the bathroom and leaned against the counter to pull on the pants. One they were secured and she was fairly certain they weren't going to fall around her ankles, she turned toward the sink to get a look at herself.

There was no mirror attached to the back of the cabinet. Someone had recently removed it, as evidenced by the light square where the paint behind it had retained its original color.

What the hell?

Confusion contorted her face in the form of a scrunched up nose. Kitty shrugged her shoulders and reached with her left hand to turn on the faucet. A splash of cold water on her face would do her good. *More like a bucket of ice water.*

At the sight of the mangled skin of her arm running from her elbow to her shoulder she froze. Her body had healed through the night, but not one hundred percent. Where the skin had knitted back together again during a shift, it had left behind shriveled and mutilated flesh. Stunned, Kitty shoved down the pants and lifted Rafe's too long shirt to discover the same situation on her skin from hip to knee. She'd been so wrapped up in her attraction to the wolf she'd hardly noticed her own body. The poison the feline bitches had tipped their claws with had left permanent markings that would never fade.

White-hot rage boiled through Kitty's veins. Her vision darkened around the edges as the feline began to take over. She snarled from deep inside, the action pulling at the wound on her face. She stopped again. Her face.

As if her body had down shifted into slow motion she lifted her hand and lightly touched her left cheek. The same rippled skin met her fingers from the corner of her eye to the side of her mouth. No. It couldn't be. The room began to spin and Kitty had to grab the edge of the counter to steady herself. This was not happening to her.

She stormed from the room and into the closet next door. There had to be a mirror somewhere in this godforsaken hellhole. She dug through stacks of clothing and some boxes thrown in the corner to no avail. Her search turned up nothing. She returned to the bathroom and pawed through the cabinets hoping a handheld had miraculously been left behind. Was this the reason the wolf rejected her? She was so hideous he'd had to hide the mirrors so he didn't accidentally see her reflection. Was she now the beast to his beauty? Great. That's all she needed. To be part of some twisted, dark fairy tale.

Her hand paused from her search. Kitty fought the despair rising inside her. When he'd had his hands all over her he'd purposely faced her away from him. Obviously so he didn't have to look at her. She hadn't realized... Until now. Slowly she pulled her arm from the cabinet and reached up to her face. Fear gripped her insides and held her back from again touching the sore area of the left side of her face. There had to be some mistake. Or maybe she was having another one of those weird dreams she couldn't wake from.

Her stomach roiled with the truth. The wave of resulting nausea took over and Kitty dropped to the floor and pounced on the toilet only seconds before she vomited, losing what little she had in her stomach. Agonized thoughts filled her brain as she considered how hideous she must be. It didn't take a mirror to know the pockets and rivulets that now lined her cheek presented a horrifying image. This couldn't be right. She'd forced the shift long enough to initiate the accelerated healing process so these scars made no sense.

Kitty struggled to her feet and stood in front of the sink staring at the blank wall for a moment before she turned on the water and dipped her head to the open stream. She swished the water back and forth while she struggled to make sense of the facts right in front of her. With her mouth rinsed, she turned off the faucet and took several steps backward until her back slammed into the wall. From there she slid to the floor and pulled her legs to her chest. She gulped air and worked hard to calm her racing heart before it beat out of control, but the scent of her wolf surrounded her. He was on her skin, on the clothes and she disgusted him. Kitty cried out as the despair embedded deep. The sight of her scarred arm made her skin crawl until she wanted to rip the offending flesh from her body.

They'd literally turned her into the hideous creature they accused her of being. They'd ruined the only thing she had going for her. Kitty lifted her head and roared, an unsettling screech that lifted her to her feet. She was damaged goods. Disgusting, horrific, and no longer good for anything. Just like her father had predicted. To someone like Rafe she'd be nothing more than a pity fuck.

The last thought broke something inside her and rage unlike anything she'd ever experienced whipped through her blood. With another cry of anguish she reached for the cabinet above the commode and ripped it from the wall. Tiny pieces of wood and ceramic showered down around her. Before all the pieces fell to the ground, she turned and ripped the towel bar from the wall and flung it where the mirror should have hung. She hissed and screamed, barely noticing that her eyeteeth poked her bottom lip until it bled. In an instant the tiny space morphed into a caged confinement and fresh desperation to escape rode Kitty's brain. With the full strength of the shifter, she threw the bar into the glass door of the shower, shattering it into a thousand tiny pieces. Jagged edges of glass rained down around her as she stood rooted to the floor until the last piece landed at her feet.

She fled from the tiny room and tried to regain her bearings. Instead of being smart and running for the outer door and the freedom she needed, Kitty thrashed through the room pulling everything from the walls and tables and flung them to the ground. Anger so hot and red filled every vein inside her body. Fully extended claws dug into the soft bedding and tore the material into one tiny strip after another. Her snarls and hisses filled the room, as did her blood as she jumped from one corner to the other.

In the midst of her rage the door burst open and Kitty pounced on the intruder. A vicious growl erupted from Rafe's mouth, distracting her from her mission for a mere moment. She recovered quickly and abandoned her attack on the man, going back to taking her wrath out on the bedroom. She spied a small club chair in the corner and sprang in its direction. With no effort at all she hoisted the bulky piece of furniture over her head and threw it in the direction of the door.

Rafe ducked and the chair crashed into the wall, splintering into several pieces before falling to the ground in a mangled heap.

"What the hell is going on? Stop this bullshit right this second," he ordered.

Kitty managed to ignore his command despite the constant pull in her brain to do as he said. Why wasn't there a mirror in this whole damn room? She twisted and turned and narrowed her eyes at the door that Rafe currently blocked.

"Don't even think about it, hell cat. You've done enough damage and you're even crazier than you look right now if you think I'm letting you tear the rest of my home apart."

She hissed and curled her back. Her feet shifted from side to side. One bite that's all she needed and he'd be out of her way forever. Blood lust rose inside her.

"So help me God, if you jump I will tie your ass to the bed and you won't get free for a week."

The menace in Rafe's threat barely penetrated the haze of anger that fueled her movements. He'd taken the mirrors away and now stared at her with such obvious animosity it stole her breath. His eyes scanned her scarred face and arm while his lip remained curled in disgust. If he wasn't going to let her out, then she wasn't going to sit by and let him gawk at her like some sort of freak. If he wanted freak, she'd give him freak.

She lifted her claws and angled them across her rippled and reddened flesh. The tip of one claw pierced the skin and blood oozed from the wound.

"What are you—?"

Before he could finish the question she started to rip and the wolf flew at her in a blur of muscles and fur. There was no time to react before he tumbled her to the bed with her arms pinned to her sides. With his full weight pressing her into the mattress, Kitty could only take short breaths. Well trained in escaping capture, she sagged into the bed, her muscles going lax. A few moments later she tested his grip and tried to slip loose. Rafe responded by growling low in her ear and tightening his hold on her wrists.

"I warned you."

In another blur of motion he produced short lengths of rope that he used to fasten one wrist to the headboard while pinning her lower half with his legs. Sweat broke out on Rafe's brow and Kitty found herself more captivated by the beads of sweat sliding down the side of his face than the fact he truly was tying her to the bed. She studied his face, admiring the angular set of his jaw, the muscle that twitched where he gritted his teeth, and the small dimple in his chin. The urge to nip the indentation flared bright and hot inside Kitty. The firm set of his lips may have indicated concentration to anyone else but to her it was like an invitation to taste his determination, an impulse almost impossible to ignore.

With enormous restraint she focused her attention lower. This close, with his body crushed to hers, she marveled at the hard planes of his chest and abs as they pressed into her. Some of the rage she'd been experiencing channeled in a different direction as his touch made her skin tingle. She breathed deep, memorizing his scent even further. The only word she could associate with him at the moment was wild, which directly conflicted with the controlled way he'd behaved every step of the way since she'd met him.

Until now...

Kitty tugged on her wrists and some of the fear and anger resurfaced. She hissed. He truly had tied her to the bed like he'd warned. At least the man followed through on his threats. Not many did these days. All her life it had been one promise or threat after another. She'd met far too many cowards in her clan, including and especially her asshole father. He'd wasted a brilliant mind with a weak will. His breeding obsession had been the death of him. A flash of anger washed over her at the memory.

"Let me up," she demanded

"I don't think so." Rafe's answer sounded gentle, but Kitty didn't miss the hint of steel underneath his drawl. Instead of pushing away from her the infuriating man straddled her hips before he pushed up, leaving her lower body as trapped as her hands. "First you're going to tell me what's got you in such a snit."

Kitty's face flushed hot and she bit her tongue. "Snit? What the hell is a snit? I'm not some junior league wolf pretending to be human. I don't know what kind of women you're used to but cougars don't do snits!" She knew the sarcasm and hysterical tone did little to help her case but the man had already made his opinion of her clear and this... this was too much.

A slow smile crossed Rafe's face. "Damn, woman. What does it take to shut you down? Less than forty-eight hours ago you were knocking at death's door and now you look like you'd kill me if given half the chance."

"Damn right," she snarled. "Survival of the fittest, wolf. It takes more than a mangy dog to put me down."

A dark cloud passed over his face seconds after she realized she'd gone too far. Her original intention to be cooperative simply to get his guard down had slipped away for good.

He bent forward, placing his nose a mere inch from hers. "I'd think twice before hurling any more insults my way. I've done nothing but offer you help, something I'm certain I'll pay for later. So the least you could do is be grateful."

Kitty laughed, a dark and twisted sound that would send a normal man running. Since Rafe didn't budge he was obviously far from normal. "I don't need your pity."

He licked his lips. "I don't do pity. I am, however, curious about what it is you need?"

"My freedom," she demanded.

His gaze only wavered for a second but Kitty didn't miss the direction. He'd glanced at her wrist, reminding her of the tattoo she now bore that confined her to the neutral zone. Just another fun reminder of her father and his schemes.

"No." His one word answer said it all.

Kitty tore her gaze from his and turned the scarred side of her face away from him. "What do you want from me? Haven't you had your fill?"

"What the hell is that supposed to mean? All I've done is help you and in return you've trashed my house and lied to me."

Exhaustion began to creep over Kitty. This conversation was leading nowhere. The big black pit of despair beckoned and it was hard not to give in.

"I didn't lie." She'd done enough lying in her lifetime and she was done. If people wanted to hear the cold, hard truth. Fine. From now on they'd get the truth.

He stared down at her, his gaze never wavering. "Yes, little cat, you did. You don't need pity nor do you *need* freedom. So what is it you *need* from me?"

Her stomach jumped. They were on a slippery slope. "Just leave me alone. I don't want to talk anymore." She rested her head into the pillow, only sensing Rafe's withdrawal. She waited for him to leave her but he didn't. Instead his fingers grasped her chin and turned her to face him. Kitty squeezed her eyes closed and prayed the threatening tears wouldn't fall.

"What happened?"

She wasn't sure where to start. How much did he need to know? She eyed him warily. The steely strength and genuine interest nearly undid her resolve. Kitty inhaled, sifting through his many layers of scents, waiting for the basic essence of the wolf to offend her. Something tightened inside her chest and a surge of fear constricted her airways. "It doesn't matter. What's done is done."

"It does matter," he insisted.

Kitty waited several heart beats, hoping he'd move on to another subject. But apparently he had the patience of a saint and the silence between them killed her resolve. "I deserved this."

"Bullshit."

She cast her gaze down. No way could she look in his eyes and say it. "It's true. I've been a rotten, conniving bitch most of my life who cared about only two things. Me and getting away from my father. I was never truly part of the clan and the women who did this were only paying me back for all the shit I did to them in one big way. Their justice may have been harsh and outside the law, but it doesn't mean they were wrong..." Her voice trailed off.

"You know what? I don't care what you did, or how awful it was. Poison is the coward's way. If your accuser can't stand up and challenge you fair and square then they aren't worth the dirt under your paws."

Kitty fought the tears welling over her eyes. Rafe was completely different from what she expected.

"Is that why you felt compelled to trash this room?" He swiveled his head in the direction of the bathroom. "And in there as well?"

She followed the direction of his gaze and at the sight of shredded toilet paper and towels littering every surface the pain of her deformation returned. Without thought, she tried to lift her hand and touch the marred side of her face to only encounter her hand trapped by his rope.

No matter. She no longer needed to touch it to feel. *Ruined.* There was no other way to call it. Ruined on the inside and now on the outside.

"You took away the mirrors. It made me mad."

A heavy sigh escaped Rafe a moment before he turned back to face her. "You're still healing. You need to give the wounds time to heal before you go worrying about how they look."

Another dark laugh burst forth. "Oh that's rich. The sight of me is so repelling you can't bear to look at me so you figure I shouldn't have to see either." Her voice rose several octaves. "Let me the fuck loose right this instant. It's time for me to leave." The hairs rose first on the back of her neck and then across her arms and legs. Her teeth and claws elongated seconds before she hissed violently in his direction.

"Calm down." He leaned forward and pinned her arms to the bed. "I have no problem looking at you, wounds and all. What should bother me, however, is the cougar inside you, but for some reason even that doesn't turn me off."

Kitty bared her teeth and lunged for his throat. She didn't want to hear his bullshit now or any time in the future. Unfortunately between the ropes binding her wrists and the arms like tree trunks pinning her, he kept her several inches from her target. She bucked her hips hoping to make him lose his balance, only to slam her sex against the unmistakable hard ridge of his very stiff erection. Her sharp intake of breath brought a smile to Rafe's face. The slow spread of his lips held as much menace as they did promise.

Oh hell. He'd found the perfect channel for her rage.

Synapses misfired in her brain as her body caught immediate fire from the contact. Her already sensitive skin grew taut and the nerve endings between her legs began to throb in time with her rapidly increasing pulse. This wasn't how she was supposed to feel. Ten minutes ago she'd been in the throes of a full-blown rage ready to tear his entire house down piece by piece if that's what it took to feel better. Now she wanted nothing more than to touch...feel this man above her.

A quiet rumble began to form in her throat. Dear God, if she started to purr she was going to kill him just to save face. Kitty bit her lips to keep the not so nice retort contained. She'd done enough damage for one day.

In a brief moment of weakness, Kitty stared into the warm brown depths of Rafe's eyes. She watched mesmerized, as the colors of his eyes changed as some of his wolf emerged. The tiny flecks of gold enlarged to meld with the brown to an intense bronze that mesmerized her. Some of the thoughts keeping her wound tight softened around the edges. Heat flared in her body and swelled through her limbs. Her brain tried to make sense of what was happening but she couldn't think beyond the longing rising in her chest and making her tingle.

The urge to rub her thighs together overwhelmed her. Unfortunately with his body pressed to hers and his hips settled between the vee of her legs, there would be no self-inflicted friction to ease the sudden need she didn't understand.

With the air charging between them, Rafe opened his mouth on a sigh and she spotted the sharp points of his canines. Images of his mouth pressed to her shoulder and those teeth sliding into her flesh flooded her mind. With a slight growl, he lowered his head and pressed his nose to her left cheek. He inhaled. The small gesture shifted something inside Kitty that scared the hell out of her. She had to get her head on straight.

"You are a beautiful woman." His voice sounded low and erratic, vibrating across her skin.

She sucked in a sharp breath at the sizzling sensation rushing over her. Her thoughts buzzed with images of naked skin and tight muscle. So much for getting her head on straight. The will to be smart slowly eroded as she fantasized about taking a taste of what this man seemed to offer. She was just about to lean forward and tease his lips into the forbidden kiss she couldn't stop dreaming of. One minute was all she needed. Just a taste...

"Uhm. Excuse me."

The sound of Rafe's doctor friend at the door broke them apart. Rafe abruptly withdrew from between her legs and eased from the bed in the blink of an eye.

"What?" The rough question left little doubt as to what they'd been about to do.

"Sorry, man. I didn't want to interrupt."

"Then you shouldn't have. Last time I checked, I've got a door." In a quick movement, the wolf untied one of the ropes at her wrist and then reached for the second.

"Yeah, one I've been knocking on for five minutes. Guess you couldn't hear me through all the hormones."

Rafe growled a not so subtle warning at his friend. "So what is so damned important that I don't warrant any privacy tonight?"

For a few moments the silence thickened in the room. "You've been summoned."

R afe finished untying Kitty in silence before turning to his omega. "How bad is it?"

"He's pissed. Tanner's been running his mouth off to anyone and everyone and Burke has had enough. He wants you two at his place yesterday so I wouldn't suggest making him wait long."

"Uhm, excuse me." Kitty pushed at his arm until he moved out of her way so she could sit up. "Anyone care to explain to me what's going on?"

Rafe shook his head. He'd hoped there'd be more time before it got to this. They still barely knew each other and yet, the woman had stirred something inside him the wolf couldn't let go of. He shifted uncomfortably to prove it. His balls ached and his dick would not go down no matter how much he willed it. They definitely needed more time.

"Your friend from the woods is looking to take you back. I'm sure he figures you've healed by now and wolves tend to get pretty possessive over their property." He shot a pointed glance at his friend.

Simon held up his hands. "Don't look at me like that. I told them she was having issues healing and put them off as long as I could."

"Is that what you call this?" She held up her arm and flaunted the rough puckered skin along her otherwise smooth flesh. "An issue?"

"Don't," Rafe warned. He really didn't want to get into this with her again.

"Whatever." She brushed his warning aside. "That reminds me. Why the hell are there no mirrors in this room?"

He shrugged. He had no intention of getting into his reasoning for removing them. The damage to her arm and side were bad enough but seeing the disfiguration of her face the first time wasn't going to go well.

She pushed past Doc and started from the room. "I don't know what you two are doing with your googly eyes and bullshit sideways glances but I don't want any part of it. Isn't it about time you released me? I've got a life to live you know..." Her voice faded into the background as she wandered to the other side of the house.

"Aren't you going to go after her?" Simon questioned.

"Give her a minute. I don't think everything I said has quite sunk in yet. Right now she's got a one-track mind and isn't going anywhere. Nor is she going to find what she's looking for."

His friend whistled. "What is going on with you? This hard-on you have for her is giving me a headache."

"Shut the fuck up and tell me what else Burke had to say."

"I'd be more worried about what he didn't say. He ordered me to bring you and the girl in and then turned silent. There's a huge storm brewing and I don't like the way it feels. Tanner has managed to scrounge up a lot of support over the last few days. There's a lot of grumbling about pack rules and shit.

ELIZA GAYLE

And the pack women are spreading all kinds of rumors about you two as we speak."

Rafe rolled his shoulders. "None of Tanner's support matters when it comes down to it. At the end of the day it's the dominant wolf who will prevail."

Doc nodded but the frown on his face deepened. Rafe doubted his friend believed him. "You worry too much."

"Someone around here has too."

Rafe ignored 's sarcasm. He could take the ribbing to a point, especially when they were alone. As long as he didn't poke too hard the wolf stayed out of it.

"Seriously?" Kitty quipped from the open door. "Your best idea was to hide all the fucking mirrors? What kind of bullshit is that?"

Simon snickered and Rafe shot him a warning glare. He wasn't as easygoing as he wanted his friend to believe. The snarky little cougar standing in his doorway had him so far on the edge it wouldn't take much to tip him over. This visit with Burke would prove to be his undoing if he didn't find some control and soon. It wouldn't take much for the Alpha to sense how much she meant to him.

148

"The kind where I don't need a hysterical female on my hands today."

Her face flushed red and he swore he could almost see her head about to blow before she even opened her mouth again.

"Hysterical? Why you..."

Instead of the verbal vitriol he expected, the cat sprung and landed claws out, piercing deep into the muscles of his chest.

"Fuuuck!" He grabbed her around the waist and found a handful of hair instead of the curves he expected. A snarl sounded at his ear a second before her mouth clamped onto his throat and the first tug of his vein served as the only warning that she'd hit gold. The little bitch could rip his throat out and there wasn't a damn thing he could do about it. She'd caught him off guard and managed to trap him. He forced his body to still and willed the wolf to stay inside. A fight now might not go in his favor. The deep wail of the cat warned him how lost in the blood lust she'd managed to get in the few seconds since she'd grabbed him.

"Jesus Christ, Rafe." Simon cried from the opposite side of the bed. The stench of his friend's fear filled the room quickly.

"Get out," he croaked. It wasn't easy to talk with a fully primed and shifted she cougar straddling his chest while she pinned him to the ground, all but daring him to move.

"But..." Simon started to protest.

The cat hissed and the other man must have gotten the message. Rafe sensed the moment his friend left the room and he'd been left alone to deal with his mate.

*Mate.*

There it was again. The primal claim that wouldn't stop beating in his head since the moment he'd found her in the woods. She had to know it. Had to feel it too. Why else would he still be alive? The intrinsic instinct of the animal knew its mate. It was the one thing that superseded all others. The continuation of the species.

He took a chance the woman still lurked close to the surface and wrapped his arms around the lithe feline body of the supple cougar. Short fur brushed the fine hairs of his arms and made his skin tingle from the top of his head, to the bottom of his feet and everywhere in between. Blood rushed to his groin, hardening his shaft and the challenge to claim he'd tried to deny began. In a way he felt helpless to stop it and in another he never wanted to. His whole life he'd wondered what it would feel like to have someone be this in tune with him--this connected. All his.

With slow, careful movements he swiped his hands down her torso and marveled at the strength he found just under the surface of her cougar's skin. Taut muscles teased as well as served as a reminder that she too was as much a predator as he, maybe more so. Felines weren't known for their pack nature like wolves. They hunted alone and often, and rarely mated for life. It was more their human DNA that held them together as a group, not the animal. That solitary nature made his kind wary of getting too close to their breeds. Their loyalty was never certain and they trusted the wolf breeds even less.

So why her and why now? The question continued to plague him despite the lingering doubts. He turned his face into her side and pressed his nose to her fur, inhaling deep. She constantly reminded him of a field of wildflowers on a hot summer day with an underlying scent of something else. He breathed again, this time deeper. Fear. Faint but unmistakable. The truth of their situation sliced deep. If they were to mate, a mix of their breeds would bring nothing but trouble. He'd seen it first hand. Which still did nothing to deter him from petting her further. The first twinge of magic from her suffused him with an intoxicating wave of arousal as the big cat in his arms turned seamlessly to the woman he desired above all else.

Fur turned to warm, fragrant skin that slid against him sinuously, teasing his senses. Instinct guided him as he stroked and touched everywhere that he could. His Kitty was scared and he didn't blame her. The best he could offer her for now was a distraction--through pleasure. Yes, more pleasure than either of them could possibly bear.

Soon the reality of their situation would crash down on them and she'd be faced with multiple issues that would threaten her life and his sanity.

A growl slid along his throat.

*Protect.*

*Fight.*

When Kitty hissed, Rafe realized he'd tightened his hand to a white knuckled grip around her arm. For fuck's sake. He would be no help to her if he couldn't even control his baser urges.

Pleasure. Focus. Give her what she needs and show her how it can be. Somehow his brain managed a few last coherent thoughts before he flipped her to the floor and came down on top of her. Her body called to him, made him want to see her submitting to both their needs. But this wasn't about control. He sensed something more important happening between them. Deeper. He wanted her to feel the same connection he did from the inside out. There was a lesson here they both needed to learn. Sometimes genetics and clan rules were meant to be broken. If only for a moment...

"You could have killed me," he bit out before bending to her shoulder and pressing his lips to her naked skin. "Why didn't you?"

She shrugged.

He didn't really want or expect an answer. There were too many emotions and issues swirling between them for that conversation. He trailed his fingers from the outside of one knee, along the curve of her hip until he spanned her side with one hand. With more reserve than he thought he possessed, he leaned forward and touched his lips to her damaged face. Her reflexive jerk did nothing to deter him as he tightened his grip on her waist and continued to caress her scar.

"Don't," she whimpered.

"Yes," he breathed. "Don't let your fear win here, Kitty. A simple scar doesn't change who you are inside."

"It's hardly simple." She started to protest and Rafe opted to change tactics, covering her mouth with his own and taking her with a kiss he felt clear to his soul and hoped she did as well. It only took a second for her to respond and open to him, allowing his tongue to tempt and explore the recess of her heated mouth.

Damn. Sweet heaven alive. He was going to go insane.

Seconds later her scent began to change. Some of the fear receded as the hunger and need she harbored took the forefront. That sweet softness of the woman who needed him pulled at Rafe's rough edges, encouraging him to continue. To go for it all. The wolf inside him pushed for what he wanted too with a long whine inside his head. He cared more about the claim, the dominance he needed to express. Nothing less than her neck bared as he plunged roughly inside her would satisfy the animal. Fortunately Rafe had enough human common sense left to know that there was far more to this than a simple claiming. There had to be. They were more than two animals coming together for mutual pleasure and need.

Whatever forces had brought her to his world had left behind more than a collection of angry scars on her skin. He wanted to focus on what she needed, what would bring her the greatest pleasure, but the intoxicating nature of her arousal flaring to life made it almost impossible for him to ignore the frenzy building inside him. He couldn't continue thinking straight much longer.

Nothing mattered now except her. Where she came from and what little their future likely held meant less than nothing as the kiss consumed him. Warmth wrapped around him, emanating from their connection. His balls tightened and the ache in his groin grew unbearable.

Before long she clung to him as she took as much from their kiss as he did. They ate at each other's mouths, unable to get enough. Long arms wrapped around his shoulders where she clung to him with surprising strength. Sharp claws scraped at his back, eliciting throaty growls he didn't hold back. They were going to burst into flames at this rate. Maybe take the whole damned cabin with them. He hoped Doc had enough sense to get the hell out.

Sharp teeth bit down on his lip and the invisible chain holding him back broke free.

With rampant thoughts of more running through his head, Rafe tore his mouth from her lips and scraped his teeth along her jaw and neckline. His entire body throbbed when he hesitated at the apex of her shoulder and neck, but he resisted. He kept his focus on pleasuring her, allowing her to forget everything that had led them to this, even for a short while. Reality for them both would intrude soon enough.

Her beautiful body beckoned and he was starved. After days of watching her recover with nothing more than instinct to fill the gaps in his mind, what else could he do? He continued his trail to the lush nipples that had poked at his chest. On first sight of the dusky hard buds, his mouth watered and his vision wavered before he covered one flushed tip and drew it into his mouth. He dragged his tongue across the small peak and her back arched. Her gasp of pleasure tore at his restraint as he mercilessly lashed her sensitive skin.

"So fucking good," he growled, ignoring the harsh tone of his voice. "I can't get enough." He returned to the elongated tip and scraped teeth and tongue as she shuddered beneath him.

"But—"

Rafe bit down until she gasped. He didn't want any arguments ruining their moment. "The only thing I need to hear right now is you begging me. Everything else can wait."

"Arrogant dog," she exclaimed, more out of breath than not.

"Bad Kitty," he replied gruffly, while settling between the vee of her legs. The moment his groin hit the comforting heat of her sex he groaned. Even more so when she laughed. She had a body for sin and a mind to challenge him. And she liked to bite. His dick hardened more. No doubt, he was in deep shit with this one.

He went back to her tits, savoring first one then the other. "I could do this all night."

"It would kill me," she admitted.

"Nah. Drive you mindless maybe. But that's the sweetest kind of torture." He pressed tighter between her thighs, loving the way her eyes widened in surprise. Before he could make another move, the scent of her wet pussy drifted over him. His body tightened as he fought for sheer willpower not to drive into her.

"We're going to regret this later," she protested. She lifted her head anyway and licked the side of his jaw.

In retaliation he nipped at the curve of her right breast until her harsh cry gave him the satisfaction he sought. No matter what she offered up in the way of protest it did nothing to assuage the need for her still overwhelming him. Somewhere in the back of his mind, a small voice tried to remind him of their differences at every moment but he simply ignored it for now. Maybe once he got this out of both their systems they could face the reality of the situation. Although if Burke thought he'd simply hand her over to Tanner he had another thing coming.

Alpha or not, Rafe would do whatever it took to protect what belonged to him now. And like it or not, she did belong to him.

With more than a little reluctance, Rafe released Kitty and withdrew from between her legs. At this moment he detested the clothes that separated him from her. Without finesse, he peeled his T-shirt over his shoulders and tossed it to the side. Her gaze locked onto his pecs and he watched her inspect him from shoulder to waist. He paused before unbuckling his pants, letting her look her fill before he continued. The admiration and heated lust shining in her eyes more than compensated for his patience. He'd bet she hadn't even noticed that while she stared at him, her legs had parted farther and moisture now glistened along her folds. His mouth watered at the feast before him. Torturing him. Finally he gave in and tore the button from his pants in his haste to get free.

She started to move toward him.

"No, stay just like that," he ordered.

Her body froze for a few tense seconds before she relaxed back and opened her legs with a wicked grin on her face. Rafe was pretty sure he'd never seen anything fucking prettier in his life and if he didn't get inside her soon he would simply die on the spot. He gripped himself and moved once again between her parted thighs. He used his free hand to stroke her from knee to pussy in a slow, exaggerated caress.

When the muscles of her inner thigh trembled under his touch, Rafe held back his smile. Her responsive body practically sang to him like a siren call leading her prey to exactly the spot she wanted him.

"Lie still." He spanned his left hand around her slender thigh and pinned her in place. He needed her so bad right now, but more importantly he had to explore and give her the time she needed to let go of the last shreds of her restraint. Whatever it took to have her writhing and begging he would do. He had to.

Damn, she had gorgeous curves. He used his other hand to skim her hip, admiring the wide flare before it tapered to her tiny waist. Of course there was no denying that the treasure between her thighs beckoned his gaze. Rafe pushed his fingers into the nest of neatly trimmed curls that accentuated the pink lips and parted them with two fingers. Her small gasp prodded him to continue. He watched her eyes flutter and darken as he slid one finger inside her and nearly lost his own mind at the scorching heat. Fucking A. Immediately he added a second finger. Hot silk. It was all his mind registered.

Her back arched and a cry echoed around the room. His dick jerked at the enticing sound. He withdrew his fingers. "Cry again for me, baby." He plunged both fingers inside her again and reveled in the sounds she rewarded him with. Dear God, he loved a loud woman.

He moved his fingers along tender nerve endings as her hips jerked and more of him slipped inside her. He growled, unable to stay silent. As good as she felt on his hand, it was a more important body part that ached to plunge inside her.

The scent of her aroused body flooded his senses as more, rough growls erupted in his throat. The man was losing control to the animal far too quickly. Tight, slick walls and an eager woman yearning for more would do that to any man, but a shapeshifter was a far more dangerous creature. As someone who lived amazingly close to his animalistic side, the desire to go all caveman on Kitty rode him like a demon on a mission from hell.

Her heat alone threatened to burn him alive. He twisted his fingers and sought the soft patch below her pubic bone. When she jerked against him he smiled, satisfied he'd found what he was looking for.

"You don't play fair," she gasped.

He leaned down and nipped her chin. "You got that right. There is nothing fair about what is happening between us. But right here, right now, you will enjoy everything I have to give. Period."

He was a man with no other choice than to complete what he'd started and see to his mate's pleasure above all else. Rafe shook his head. These were not the thoughts of a rational man. He had a sense these bouts of insanity when it came to his shapeshifting cougar weren't going away after this. The scent of her arousal alone affected him like a drug. He would be addicted and nothing or no one would stop him.

He grasped his erection and positioned it next to his fingers a moment before he removed them. He imagined her walls stretching to accommodate more of him and his head spun. Her cry of distress was like music to his ears, bringing him back to the moment. Now she only needed to beg and he'd come in an instant.

Rafe nudged her drenched curls with the tip of his cock until it bumped against her protruding clit. He didn't need to see the blood engorged nub to know how ready she was for him. His head dipped and pressed his lips to the shell of her ear. "Tell me, Kitty. Tell me what you want and it's yours," he whispered.

"I—I," she gasped, dragging in much needed air. "Can't think. Just need." She panted.

"Need what? Just say it. If you want it then I have to hear it." His insides trembled with the restraint it took not to plunge deeply. He wanted the words just as badly as the flesh. Maybe more.

"Don't make me say it," she choked, her legs and arms trembling.

"You have to. It's the only way." When the words were not forthcoming he began to pull away.

She righted her hands until her nails dug deep into his skin. "Do it, you bastard. Please," she begged. "Fuck me!"

The invisible vise holding Rafe together shattered as he jerked his hips forward and pushed inside her in one solid thrust. He held still and fought to breathe. "Kitty..." he groaned. His body shook. Molten silk had wrapped around him and he couldn't bear to move and take it away. Pulses of sensation skidded up and down his spine and tingled in his groin. The bliss of her body connected to his amazed him. As clichéd as he knew it to be, all he could think was that it had never in his life been this good.

Her inner muscles tightened on him at the same time her claws began to shred the sheets beneath them. Kitty shook her head and her soft blonde hair caressed his chest and arms. The nirvana of this moment imprinted on his memory. With any luck the sensation of his mate's pleasure would sustain him through the coming dark nights.

Unable to hold still another moment, Rafe pulled his shaft from the clenching depth of her pussy until only the head remained and immediately began working inside her again. Slow and steady this time, he pushed through muscles so tight he thought his head would explode.

"Am I hurting you?"

"Yes. No. I don't know. Fuck. Don't stop," she exclaimed.

He clenched his jaw and pressed forward, pulled back and gave her more. The constant stream of whimpers and cries as she thrashed from side to side unraveled his own reservations. He needed to be buried inside his mate so far she'd never accept another man. Never forget this moment.

Shit, who was he kidding? The scars of tonight were already embedded in his psyche. When things went to shit, and they would, it was his sanity that would be lost. "Do you want more?" He plunged into her with deep, punishing strokes before she answered. Hard jabs that pushed her into the mattress.

"Yes!" she screamed.

A strangled cry followed and he lifted his head to the night sky visible through the glass ceiling. The moon called to him, gave him strength. The growl that had been building erupted into a full-blown howl and was met by a vicious banshee like scream from Kitty. Her muscles clenched around him and pulled him into the abyss she'd already fallen into.

"Oh shit, going to come!" Every muscle in his body clenched and exploded. Hard jets of cum emptied into his mate and still she continued to milk him with her muscles tightening in short, powerful pulses. When he was finished, he continued to thrust. Thoughts of complete and utter possession filled his mind. After giving up hope of finding her, he was finally with his born mate. Their now commingled scent drifted to his senses, driving him mad. Kitty. He gazed down at her face. Her eyelids were closed, her mouth slightly parted as she tried to breathe. All he saw was the pure unadulterated beauty of his mate. The moon bathed her skin in light while a firestorm of emotions and sensations shot through him in a shocking wave his brain didn't know how to process. His little Kitty had destroyed him.

Rafe collapsed next to her on the bed, the tattered sheets a reminder of their loss of control. They both fought for air as their heartbeats slowed to normal. He pulled her tight to his chest and buried his nose in her hair. The urge to bite and claim still rode him pretty hard but somehow, some way he would find a way to resist a second time.

For the first time in his life he didn't know what to do. The animal instincts he easily controlled on a daily basis now rode him for a change. The wolf beckoned and if he tried to ignore him for too long, all hell would break loose. So much for letting go.

"Rafe?"

He turned and nuzzled her hair. "Mmm hmm," he responded.

"Do you have any food? I'm starving."

CHAPTER
# ELEVEN

R afe laughed. "Oh look, the pretty little Kitty has worked up an appetite."

She punched him in the arm. "Smart ass. If you don't want to feed me just say so." The shit-eating grin on her face said it all.

He was certainly hungry but it wasn't for food unless what was between her legs counted. Despite the mind-blowing orgasm they'd just shared, he ached for more. His appetite for sex with this woman could easily border on insatiable.

But her needs came first and she'd barely recovered from a life-threatening ordeal. Of course she needed food. "Who am I to deny you anything that you need." He pressed a quick kiss to her mouth and stood from the bed. "Simon is still here so unfortunately you'll need these." He bent and picked up her discarded clothes. As she grabbed them and immediately shoved her legs into the pants and began tying the waist and rolling up the pant legs, he couldn't keep quiet any longer. "I have to admit of all the clothing choices the pack ladies brought by, I'm surprised to see you chose a pair of my pants to wear."

She stared at him, a solemn look in her eyes. "A few days ago I would have hated these. I would have wanted the frilliest or skimpiest clothing I could find."

"And now?"

"I'm not the same person I was a few days ago, now am I?" Her gaze shifted away from him.

His heart squeezed at the sadness in her voice. He snagged her around the waist and tilted her head to face him. "I didn't know you a few days ago so I couldn't comment on that. But I'm growing damn fond of who you are now and if you want to wear my pants every day that's fine by me. I will enjoy it twice as much when I peel them off you."

Her mouth opened and closed like she'd started to say something and changed her mind. "C'mon let's eat." He grabbed his clothes and they finished dressing quickly before heading toward the main area of the house. "I've got a fully stocked kitchen so you name it and I'm sure we can figure something out."

"Do you have any frozen pizza? That would really hit the spot right now."

He turned to face her and froze as Kitty slammed into his back. He grabbed her arm and kept her from falling. "Did you really just ask for frozen pizza?"

She scrunched her face. "Well, yeah... It's my favorite. It's easy, it tastes good and perfect for someone who doesn't like to cook."

"You don't like to cook?"

"Nope. That female gene skipped right over me. Although it's not for the lack of my father trying to force me to learn. Thankfully, after about three dozen ruined meals, he gave up. It's been takeout and frozen meals ever since."

He had a bad feeling that forcing her to learn to cook was the least of her father's crimes. If she thought she deserved what was done to her by those feline bitches it's because she'd learned her bad behavior from the king of bastards. Rafe pulled her against his chest and reveled in the heat and scent of his mate.

"You're out of luck in the frozen anything department in this house." Simon's words interrupted Rafe's train of thought. "Rafe here fancies himself a chef and if anyone dared to bring something less than natural and organic into his house, he'd likely bite them."

Her head tilted up until their gazes met and held. "Bite, huh?"

"Yes. Would you like a personal demonstration?" He leaned forward and licked behind her ear before scraping his teeth across the silky flesh.

"We don't have time for this. Have you forgotten that you've been summoned?"

Simon was fast becoming a serious pain in his ass. With great reluctance he pulled away from Kitty and turned to his friend. "I think Burke can wait long enough for us to feed our patient. She's had little more than fluids since she's arrived and she's hungry." He was too. Starved actually, but it wasn't food he needed. This scrappy, ready to fight or run woman had awakened his sex drive and ramped it up to the tenth power.

"Well then, by all means feed her. But make it quick. Burke's going to have both our heads on a roasting stick at this rate."

Rafe looked at Kitty and rolled his eyes. "You'll have to excuse Simon and his flair for the over dramatic. I think that last female he had in his bed must have stolen his balls."

"Yeah, fuck you, buddy." Simon glared daggers at him and Rafe only laughed.

"Simon's not happy with me. He's a lover, not a fighter."

"Yeah, and you blowing off Burke is going to get both our asses kicked."

Rafe chose to ignore Simon's words and pulled Kitty into the kitchen. "Maybe you only think you can't cook because no one has ever taught you properly."

She wrinkled her nose at him. "Why? Is it so hard to believe that a woman wouldn't feel at home in a kitchen? Are all your pack females running barefoot in their kitchens?"

Simon snorted. "Hardly. The men do most of the cooking in the pack. We're short on females so they tend to be busy doing other things."

Rafe glared daggers at his friend and willed him to shut the hell up. He cupped Kitty's face to distract her from Simon and his idiocy. "If you have no interest in cooking, then that's cool. Just sometimes the right teacher makes all the difference in the world." He waggled his eyebrows suggestively.

"I'm starting to understand why you're still single," she said with a smirk on her face.

Rafe clutched his heart. "Ouch."

She shrugged in response.

"Fine," he led her to one of the stools at the bar and lifted her in place. "You can sit there and watch while I whip something up." He turned and opened the refrigerator, looking for the red sauce he'd made a couple of days ago. "This should be just right now that it's had time to sit."

He pulled out pots and pans and disappeared into the huge walk-in pantry he'd custom built when he designed his new home. With all the ingredients he needed in hand, he returned to the kitchen and set about making some amazing pasta. Frozen pizza my ass.

"Once you get a taste of his red sauce, I doubt you'll ever again settle for anything frozen or canned."

"Maybe," she offered. "Clearly I'm not a gourmet."

"Maybe Rafe will change that about you. He has that kind of influence on a person."

"What do you mean?" she asked.

"The man has a gift for all kinds of things. Cooking, negotiating, fighting. You name it, he's good at it. That's why he's about to become our next Alpha. He's destined for greatness."

Rafe inwardly cringed at Simon's praise. If he was all that then he would have thought to put a gag on Simon before he let Kitty sit with him.

"You're going to be Alpha?" There was no mistaking the alarm in her voice when she said it.

"It's not that big of a deal. Burke is my uncle. He's ready to retire and he doesn't have any sons of his own. I'm the oldest of my brothers so that makes me first in line. Unless any of them want to fight me for it, which I don't see happening." He placed the dry linguine into the pot of boiling water and added a dash of olive oil. He had seven to eight minutes to calm Kitty's fears before he could distract her with his food.

"How many brothers do you have?"

"Just two. They should be back soon. They were sent out to some neighboring packs to discuss uh—pack relations." He didn't think she was ready to hear they were actually trying to barter an arranged mating.

"I REALIZE I don't know a thing about pack politics, but I don't believe you that becoming Alpha is no big deal. You can't— I mean, we can't— This is bad."

She didn't have to finish either of those statements. He knew exactly what she meant. "You think because I'm a wolf and you're a cougar that we can't—"

"Stop. Please, just don't say it. Even saying the words will damn us both."

"I think I'm going to get some fresh air and make some phone calls. I have a few patients I need to check up on." Finally Simon got with the program.

Neither of them said another word until the front door closed behind his friend. He picked up Kitty's hand and closed his fingers around it.

"Don't tell me you can't feel what's going on between us. We both damn well understand our DNA."

"That doesn't mean we don't have any other choices. I'm going to guess your pack wants you to mate with a cougar about as much my clan would welcome a wolf."

Rafe turned her hand over and ran his thumb across the small mark at her wrist. "If this is what your clan did to you, then you have no need to go back there. Thanks to them you almost died." Her breath hitched at his continued touch. Heat spread like wildfire inside him because of it.

"And what about your pack? Are they going to welcome me with open arms?"

"I honestly don't know." He took a deep breath, letting her scent calm him. "Not everyone agrees with the old fashioned beliefs that we should only mate with other wolves. Like Simon said, our female numbers have dwindled and this might be nature's way of fixing that."

She pulled her hand free. "I'm not your savior, Rafe."

"But you are my mate."

This time she rolled her eyes at him. "Just because every time you touch me my stomach rolls doesn't mean we have to give in to this born mate nonsense. We are still human. Some of us a little more than others."

"What's that supposed to mean?" He was starting to feel some of his tightly held control slip away.

"Nothing, Rafe." She sighed. "The Alpha of your pack deserves more than a damaged feline who struggles to hold a shift," she whispered.

He stilled. Part of him wanted to wring her neck for suggesting a few scars should make a difference to any man worth his title, but the last part of her statement finally sunk in.

"What do you mean you struggle to hold the shift? You didn't tell us that the poison had gone beyond the surface like that."

"It didn't. I've been like that for as long as I can remember. I kept it a secret because I was afraid what my father or my clan would do to me if they found out I was defective."

"Defective?" Anger so hot rushed through Rafe's body, nearly melting his brain. "That's ridiculous. Differences don't make us defective. They make us individuals." The notion that a father had hurt his child even emotionally with his wild theories and insistence on all perfect offspring served as the ideal reminder why he had to become the Alpha. It was time someone took a stand against species purity once and for all.

Before he could argue the point, his internal timer went off and he had to return to the stove. While his mind processed all the things he needed to accomplish and how much more effectively it could be done with Kitty by his side, he drained the pasta, transferred it to a bowl and dished up a plate for his mate.

"Here, try this. And then tell me if you still crave your frozen pizza." He placed the dish in front of her and stood back to watch. Already the tantalizing scents of Italian herbs and garlic filled the room and he anxiously waited for her to be blown away.

She twirled the pasta on her fork and then lifted it to her mouth. Their eyes met and her mouth pursed to blow on the steaming food. His body reacted immediately and the wolf inside him whined. Again, the thoughts of what she could do with that mouth flooded through him. She opened wide and slowly slid the fork inside before wrapping her lips around the tines and sucking the noodles free. Rafe gulped. All the blood in his body rushed to his groin. She wasn't just eating his food, she was toying with him.

"Mmm." Her eyes closed and her face slackened. "This is really good."

Rafe sat mesmerized as he watched her eat the entire plate of pasta. Between the licking of her lips, the small satisfied moans, and the fact she was really loving his food, it was difficult to stand still. The animal inside strained at the leash Rafe had put him on, but the human urges weren't any easier. He really liked her and it wasn't just about the mate thing. Those scars didn't take anything away from her beauty. They simply made her more real. Of course that didn't mean he wasn't itching to hunt down the people who'd hurt her and mete out a little wolf justice.

Between the rumors he'd heard about her and what little she'd provided so far, he knew she came with quite a past. Even better. There was no time like the present for her to make a fresh start with him. Her background would give her the backbone and means to be an Alpha's mate. The last thing he needed was some society wolf who thought of nothing else but how to raise her rank in the pack.

"Rafe. Earth to Rafe. Did you hear a word I said?"

He jerked from his thoughts and focused in on her gaze. "What? No. Sorry."

She shook her head at him. "I was saying we should probably go now."

He zeroed in on her lips. "Uh uh." He came around the kitchen peninsula and pulled her from the stool. "First I want this." He pushed his fingers through her hair at the nape of her neck and smashed his mouth down on hers, swallowing her stunned gasp.

Their tongues tangled and her arms wrapped around his waist. God, he loved her touch, her taste. How could he let their differences come between them now and lose this? He didn't care that it had only been a few days. Some things just are.

He pushed his hands up her full hips and past the lovely indentation of her waist. There was so much more to enjoy from a woman like her.

In classic bad Simon timing, the front door began to rattle. They sprung apart, panting for air.

"I guess we have to go," she said.

"Yes. We're going to have to explain to Burke that we're mates."

A look of pure horror crossed Kitty's face. "Like hell. You can't throw your entire future away over this."

"She's right, of course." Simon entered the room. He held up his hand. "Wait. Hear me out before you start planning my death. Burke's going to smell the two of you coming a mile away so he'll figure it out easy enough. I mean seriously." He waved his hand in front of his face. "But if we don't get there until the moon is high and the rest of the pack is too focused on the coming hunt, you'll give Burke an opportunity to decide what to do without forcing his hand. He can be a little old guard sometimes but you know he supports your politics. I think you should trust him to do the right thing."

Rafe relaxed back on his heels and thought about what Simon said. He couldn't stomach having to choose between his mate and pack and if there was a way to keep them both then that's the path he had to pursue. Would Burke make the right decision when he sensed what had happened? It'd be a lot better if Rafe had marked her a little more permanently, but he had a feeling making that suggestion would not go over well at the moment.

"I vote for letting the chips fall where they may before anyone else gets into a fight," Kitty added

Rafe grasped her shoulders and pulled her closer. "Do you trust me that I won't let Tanner hurt you no matter what happens?"

"Uhm, sure," she answered.

Not that her doubt didn't broadcast loud and clear, but he'd take it for now. Burke was family but that didn't always trump pack. One way or another he'd keep Kitty safe, even if that meant walking away.

# CHAPTER
# TWELVE

Kitty valiantly tried to cling to her tattered dignity as she trailed behind Rafe and Doc through the woods. On the thirty-minute drive from Rafe's house, they'd all sat silently as his pickup truck drove deeper and deeper into the woods. From paved streets to barely a gravel road no one had said a word. Tension was thick and she didn't know what to do about it.

What had she been thinking? Sex with a wolf was a sure recipe for trouble and now they'd pay. She shook her head. She wasn't thinking. That was the problem. Or at the very least she'd decided to ignore all common sense. Her instincts seemed to go haywire any time Rafe got near her.

What a fucking dumbass. She'd allowed her pity party and a few hormones to drown her normally rigid self control. It wouldn't happen again. It couldn't.

Still, the memory of her wolf staring down at her with nothing that resembled pity wrapped around her mind. Every time he'd peeled his lips back and bared his teeth she'd braced for the bite. Part of her wanted to be marked as much as he'd been tempted to do it. He hadn't said as much, but the knowledge had been in his eyes and the way they continued to stare at her bare neck.

Kitty wanted to wipe the memories away and forget the last several days ever happened. It simply wasn't possible she was falling for *him*.

Of course, then he'd gone and cooked for her. No one had ever done anything like that for her. Even with Simon sitting there most of the time it had felt like a date, another new experience for her. She'd been off kilter and greedy for more the entire time. Sex she understood and if she was lucky sometimes it came with a few nice words. This nearly uncontrollable desire to be with Rafe, on the other hand...

Now he was ready to sacrifice everything for her and she refused to allow it. She agreed with Simon about his destiny for greatness. He'd taken in the fact that his potential mate wasn't a wolf and run with it. Hell, he appeared to embrace it. If he had his way he'd have locked her in his house and she'd be barefoot and pregnant before she knew it. Not many people she knew would do the same. *More like nobody.*

Now it was up to her to make sure for once in her life she did the right thing for someone other than her.

After a short fifteen-minute walk from where they'd left the truck, the three of them arrived on Alpha property and were met by no less than a half a dozen guards.

"You've kept him waiting," one of them spoke directly to Rafe while the others slowly edged closer to her.

"It's none of your fucking business who I keep waiting. We were summoned and now we're here." Rafe bared his teeth and waited. She could feel the tension in the air. There were definitely going to be some dominance issues tonight.

The tall guard turned an angry shade of red and hesitated for several long seconds before he stepped back from Rafe and dropped his head. Kitty let out the breath she'd been holding and ogled the men in front of her. These men were very unhappy with Rafe at the moment but still managed to acknowledge his status. She didn't exactly understand much about pack politics since she'd learned very little second hand. But the law of the jungle was an instinct she understood well. Survival of the fittest and submit to the alpha animal or risk death. Even humans understood the concept. Whoever held the power maintained control.

Rafe was an alpha and these were not. He might not be pack alpha but he held a much higher rank in their pecking order. Now she wished she'd taken some time to ask more questions. How much power he maintained would have a lot to do with her fate. Despite the chill in the air, a sheen of sweat broke out across her brow. Healed fully or not she was on the verge of running. Her cat was restless and skittish. If things continued into danger, she'd push the human aside and take control.

Kitty followed Rafe inside a large barn and immediately stopped moving. The scent of wolf overwhelmed her. Her body jerked and her hand came up to cover her nose and mouth. Rafe whirled in her direction and grabbed her around the waist pushing her back out the door and turned them both until her back hit the side of the barn and he covered her body with his.

He leaned into her hair and whispered. "Control your responses. Any sudden moves or reactions will be taken as a sign of weakness and an already impossible situation will get worse." His hands roamed her sides and his fingers tightened on her hips. She started to object when she realized what he was doing. He'd pulled her to the side in the guise of some sort of sexual move so that no one would notice her reaction.

"Seriously, Kitty. I get how you feel right now. But your life may very well depend on how you handle yourself in there. They'll be looking for any and all weaknesses they can exploit. Got it? If Burke doesn't believe in you then we've got nothing."

She nodded. Her stomach rolled and her eyes burned from the overload of scents stealing through her, but the determination to appear strong fought for dominance inside her. "This isn't my first dog and pony show," she finally bit out. "I can take it."

Rafe lifted his head and looked down at her, the sides of his mouth twitching as if fighting a smile. He pushed himself off the wall and took a step back, giving her a few more inches to breath. "Might want to tone down the sarcasm too." He lifted his hand and cupped her cheek. "While I find it sexy as hell, they might not."

She didn't mean to turn into his hand but she couldn't help herself. His touch was magnetic and sensual. The man had a dangerous knack for calming her. She wasn't so sure she wanted to be tamed by him.

"You're thinking too hard. Trust me to handle this and with any luck it won't have to get ugly."

Kitty wanted to believe him but trust wasn't exactly her strong suit. "Maybe. Or maybe I should take my chances and run now."

The look in his eyes sharpened. "Running is out of the question. You want to start a statewide cat hunt? You don't stand a chance on your own against the whole pack so get that idea out of your head right now. You're mine to protect."

The rough edge of his voice with a heavy dose of possessiveness startled her. Part of her wanted to argue with him and the other melted a little. The two separate thought processes were going to drive her mad.

"We'll see. But I don't relish pissing off your entire pack today so let's just do this." She brushed past him and tried not to think about how good he'd felt inside her or how badly she'd wanted him to bite her when he came. This wasn't the time or place for her head to be in the clouds. Her life depended on what she did next.

Inside the door, her eyes scanned the room. Where she'd been expecting an actual barn where maybe animals are kept, she found something totally different. It looked more like the inside of a modern recreation center than a barn. Except the smell. This many wolves together created a stench she wasn't used to. She forced herself to breath through her mouth and not give away any visual signs of her reaction. Inside though was a whole 'nother story. As all of the talking ceased and everyone turned to look at her, her insides churned with unease.

"What the hell is that?" A young good looking man approached her, his teeth bared in a snarl and closely followed by a low growl.

Kitty stood her ground. She curled her hands into fists at her sides and hissed in his direction. Several men surrounded her but it was Rafe's touch on her arm that caught her attention. He wanted her to trust in him but she didn't know if she could. It simply felt like too much for him to ask.

"Bout time you brought her to me." She heard the booming voice from the back of the room and a chill ran up her spine. Her memories from that first night were still fuzzy but she recognized the sneer in his words. He'd been one of the three men who'd found her before Rafe. Most of the men in the room had gathered close by and there was a commotion in front of her as whoever had spoken broke through the crowd.

Big and tall, the man in question stopped several feet in front of her. She stared at him, trying to remember this man looming over her. Dark hair, dark beard, and eyes shining gold the longer she stared at him. Not exactly the ugly, scary man she'd imagined him to be. His sneer of contempt didn't exactly enhance his looks, but he had a look in his eye that told her not to be fooled by his demeanor.

"Glad to see you finally cleaned up." Rafe spoke from behind her as the grip on her arm tightened and he pulled her toward him until her back grazed his chest. She tried to hide the shiver his touch created, but the other man's eyes narrowed and she suspected he hadn't missed her reaction.

"Time to hand her over. My rights to *it* have already been filed and witnessed."

Kitty's muscles tensed at his reference to her as an it and she started to open her mouth and tell him where he could stick his *it*. Rafe wrapped his fingers into the waistband of her pants and the now familiar spark between them caught her attention. He sure knew how to make it difficult to concentrate.

She shook her head and tried to take in all of the wolves around her. There were different waves of growling as the man in front of her demanded she be handed over. In the midst of the commotion another man entered the fray.

Several of the men and women around her took several spaces back, including the man trying to make a claim. The air sizzled through the room, making the fine hairs at the back of her neck stand up for attention. It was easy to recognize the sensation of power. The man now moving closer had to be the pack alpha. For what felt like endless minutes but was probably only thirty seconds, he approached before stopping in front of her. She got the sense he was waiting for her to do something. More than likely he wanted her to lower her gaze in submission, but despite Rafe's pleas to go along with this meeting, she couldn't do it.

Her father had always treated her in the same way and she swore she wouldn't do it again. Any pride or pack leader commanded a certain amount of respect and she'd accept that. But the kind of submission a wolf alpha commanded had to be earned as far as she was concerned.

The corners of his mouth quirked moments before his brow furrowed and his gaze zeroed in on something.

"Step forward," he commanded.

Kitty cringed. She'd entered the barn but purposely avoided the light. The pants and long sleeved shirt she'd borrowed from Rafe covered the scars on her body but even if she'd worn makeup it wouldn't have been enough to cover the damage on her face. Deeply rutted and mangled flesh wasn't the kind of thing a little concealer could hide.

"It's okay, hell cat," Rafe whispered in her ear. "You don't need to hide."

"Are you kidding?" she whispered back under her breath. "I'm doing my best here not to run. The last thing I need right now is a heaping helping of public humiliation."

His fingers tightened at her elbow and he leaned forward until his breath brushed her ear. "Trust me, Kitty. I know what I'm doing. Now step forward and for heaven's sake lower your eyes before you incite a riot."

She blew out a hard breath. Trust sucked. Still, there was no denying her limited choices here in this large space surrounded by these—these— Shit. How had she gotten to this point again? The one question that kept popping up in her mind every time she turned around. A little more than a month ago she'd been pondering where to go on her next vacation. Maybe the felines were right. She'd done some pretty crappy things in her life and karma was a bitch after all.

Ready to bite the bullet and get this over with, she stepped into the shaft of light and faced the pack alpha with her back ramrod straight and her gaze locked to his. A couple of the men around her gasped while others growled. Either way, the scarring on her face shocked them.

"What the fuck did you do to my property, Rafe? God dammit," the wolf from the clearing demanded in obvious outrage. If he referred to her as his property one more time...

Rafe growled and she imagined his teeth bared. "You're kidding right? She was a lot worse than this when you and the assholes you call friends were planning to fuck her to death."

The wolf Rafe had called Tanner growled and bared his teeth. "Fuck you, asshole. You had no right to take her. Consider it a favor that I allowed you to keep her this long."

A menacing sound far more dangerous than a simple growl came from Rafe. Anger radiated from him in fast vicious waves, almost taking her breath away. She understood dominance games all too well and wanted nothing to do with them. Dog eat dog and whatever. She would have laughed out loud if the thought of being caught in the middle of this fight didn't scare the crap out of her.

"You are nothing but trash that doesn't deserve to be called pack and it's high time I took care of that." Claws erupted from Rafe's fingers and his skin gave way to fur. His face elongated and his muscles grew. Her eyes widened in shock at what she was seeing. The half shifted man now standing in front of her resembled neither human nor wolf. He'd become a beast.

"Enough." The command startled her. She'd been so caught up in Rafe's transformation she'd forgotten about the alpha. Another rush of power filled the room and even she had to fight the urge to bow her head. "I'll decide who get's to do what tonight, is that clear?"

Both men slowly backed down and nodded, but the violence between them didn't dissipate. Clear as day, it simmered at a full boil inside both men. For the first time in days her cougar fought for control. Instead of the effort it normally took to shift, her body threatened to give way to the demand of the animal and its desire to protect her mate.

"Look at what he did to her. She's ruined." Tanner turned and faced her. "Why the hell is she not healed?" Kitty had to bite her tongue to refrain from calling him Captain Obvious. Either his IQ fell somewhere in the lower level basement or his flair for the dramatic had robbed him of all common sense.

"Doc said whoever attacked her used a particularly nasty poison. Is that your new M.O., Tanner? Can't get a bitch to give you the time of day so you have to resort to this?"

"Hell no. What you saw is how we found her. We didn't even touch her before you showed up."

"Only because I interrupted your sick idea of a party," Rafe spat.

The Alpha shot Tanner a hard look and stopped the other man from another outburst. "I've heard more than my fill from Tanner and his witnesses." He turned to Rafe. "Now it's time to hear what you have to say and it better be damned good. You've been avoiding me. Why?"

"Not avoiding, per se. Doc and I have been treating our patient. There wasn't much cause to address Tanner's ridiculous claim when her life hung by a thread. Whatever that poison is, it did a number on her."

"She couldn't shift and heal? Even if I hadn't been briefed on her species, I can smell it all over her." He'd curled his lip as he'd spoken. Like it or not, this is the kind of reaction they'd get from every wolf. Their DNA had been hard wired to avoid other predatory species.

Doc stepped forward, flanking her right. "So far I haven't been able to identify the poison. Whatever it is, it was meant to be fatal."

Kitty jerked her head in Simon's direction. She'd known that to be the case, but the finality of his words shocked her.

"As for the shift. She's done so many times over the last several days and while it saved her life, it wasn't enough to fix everything."

Again Kitty's stomach cramped. These weren't just scars. They were mangled flesh reminders of all the shitty things she'd done in her life and the bitches who'd sought to set their world right. After she'd fought through a lot of anger she'd had to admit they weren't one hundred percent wrong.

"I don't believe them. Whatever happened, happened while he hid my property up there on his booby trapped mountain. I ain't stupid you know."

"Come here." The Alpha motioned for her to move closer.

She didn't want to. With every eye in the room fixed on her and the disapproving and downright hostile looks being thrown her way, the only thing she wanted to do was escape. Freedom.

"Go ahead, Kitty. Trust me, remember?" Rafe's low rumbled words slid over her, working through her like a balm to her frazzled nerves. "I trust Burke and you can too."

She stared at Rafe for a few long minutes and got lost in the depths of his now glowing eyes. She didn't trust anyone, but in this case she had no other choice. She did as instructed and walked within touching distance to the leader of this wolf pack.

He focused on her gaze. "I can't decide whether you're skittish or just plain defiant. Either way it's time to move on with this show." He reached up and gripped her chin and turned her face so he could examine the mangled half of her face. The power innate to a man of his level sizzled through her. Not as electric as Rafe's touch but a constant reminder that he had the power to free her or crush her.

"Are you still in pain?"

She shook her head. "It hurt like hell when it happened, but since Rafe rescued me I've had time to heal."

"Any reason I shouldn't honor Tanner's claim on you?"

Automatically Kitty's gaze shifted to Rafe's for a second or two before she realized what she'd done and she quickly averted her eyes. If they suspected that something more than caregiving had gone on between them, the pack could turn against them both. "I understand that I broke the treaty by crossing over into your territory without permission or escort, but I was running for my life. Are there no exceptions for extenuating circumstances?"

The intimidating stare continued for a few seconds more before he turned and faced Rafe. "What do you have to say about this situation, nephew? Are there extenuating circumstances?" The two men stared at each other and Kitty got the feeling she'd walked into some power struggle that had nothing at all to do with her appearance on their land.

Kitty glared at Rafe and willed him to turn her way or catch a glimpse of her. Whatever it took to get the message across that he had to keep his mouth shut.

Whatever punishment short of death this wolf wanted to inflict on her was better than him sacrificing everything with the truth.

Apparently Tanner wasn't enjoying the strange power struggle either. "What extenuating circumstances? How many times do I have to say it? I found her. Pack law states first come, first serve. That makes her mine to do with as I see fit." He curled his lip and nodded in her direction. "Even if she's damaged goods, she should still be able to fuck."

Rafe exploded. His lips curled back and he swung his arm at Tanner's head. If the pack leader hadn't caught his wrist mid strike, she imagined Tanner would be on the ground bleeding out. What an ass.

"Pull yourself together before you blow everything," the older man growled at Rafe, low enough that only the two of them heard him. "I tell you what." He turned and faced the pack. "Since my nephew doesn't seem to have anything else to say and they're both hell bent on fighting over this girl, then we're going to do this old school."

Murmurs erupted in the crowd and Kitty's stomach plummeted to the ground. She had no idea what that meant but her experience with her clan's ancient laws and the building excitement amongst all the wolves didn't bode well for whatever this alpha considered old school.

"I'm calling for a good old-fashioned chase and capture. I'll give her a ten minute head start and whoever catches her first wins. Agreed?"

"Hell no," Tanner objected. "Pack law states—"

The old man turned and rumbled in response. "If you try to quote pack law to me one more time I'm going to put you down myself. I'm the master here and what I say goes." He crossed his arms and raised his eyebrows. "Unless of course, you're willing to challenge me right here, right now."

Kitty practically saw steam coming from the other man's ears but he wisely kept his mouth shut.

"What are the rules?" Rafe asked.

"Rules are for pussies. She runs, then y'all run her down. The winner decides what to do with her. I don't care how it happens but no one leaves these woods tonight until this shit is settled. Am I clear?"

Men and half-beasts erupted into a series of grunts and howls that made the walls of their community center barn shake. She spied blood lust in many of their eyes as they stared at her like the prey she'd just become. A big bay door in the back rolled up and everyone began to undress. Some neatly folded their clothes and left them in a pile while others were too far gone in their shifts to do little more than rip through the impeding fabric.

Rafe pulled her toward him and bent his head to her ear. "When he says go, you need to get outside, shift and run like fucking hell. Don't look back and don't wonder if anyone is close. Just run. If you head straight east you're only about fifteen miles from the neutral zone. Most of the pack won't dare touch you if you make it that far."

Kitty swallowed. "Most?"

His grip tightened on her bicep. "Do you trust me to keep you safe?"

Did she? As much as she'd enjoyed the past few days with him, they hadn't wiped out a lifetime of mistrust still messing with her head. "I'm okay with this," she admitted. "This gives me a chance and that's all I care about." That wasn't exactly the whole truth but in light of his pack salivating for her blood it seemed the smart thing to say.

"I'll catch you," he said with a low rumble in his voice. "And when I do no more running. You'll be mine...forever."

The word forever reverberated through her head. In light of her predicament, forever seemed like a very short timeframe.

The leader lifted his head and let loose with a long, loud howl that whipped the rest of the pack into more of a frenzy. Rafe wanted to keep her safe but in the face of a hundred or more wolves, the odds were against him. Before Rafe could say another word, the alpha turned to her with his eyes gleaming red and yelled, "Run!"

The force of his command slammed into her and the cat screamed. Instinct kicked in and she turned and did exactly as he insisted.

Hair erupted along her skin as she moved and her face and teeth began to change. Outside the building with the sound of wolves howling and growling in anticipation of a kill, she tore at her clothes and shifted.

Bones and muscles popped more than normal and Kitty was forced to bear a higher level of pain than

# CHAPTER
## THIRTEEN

*S* *hit*. He hoped to God she heard what he'd said. He'd seen the moment her inner animal had taken control and he had no idea how lucid she'd remain while running for her life. At least she'd taken off in the direction he'd indicated.

The ten-minute head start she'd been given felt like hours. He watched the clock tick down constantly and barely contained the overriding urge to go after his mate.

He had to follow the rules through this or they'd both be fighting for their lives. Easier said than done when all he could smell despite more than half the pack filling the community center was her. The wild scent of the woman had gotten into his head and nothing else could replace it. *Mate.*

The word now taunted him day and night. Rafe breathed deeply and focused on Kitty. He'd given up the fight the moment she turned those pretty green eyes on him, followed by the moment she'd hinted that she trusted him. She had no business trusting him after what she'd been through, but whether she saw it or not there was an innate goodness inside her just waiting to be drawn out. A job he looked forward to if he had to do it with her kicking and screaming the whole way.

He snarled low in his throat. She needed him and he couldn't stand here and do nothing.

"Two minutes and then you can go," his uncle stated. The man had stayed by his side. Probably not as a show of support though. More likely he'd expected to have to stop him from running immediately after her.

"You're a bastard. There had to have been another way."

One of the nearby unshifted wolves lifted his brow.

"Careful what you say to me young un. I'd hate to have to make an example of you in front of the entire pack."

Rafe bristled at Burke's words. There was no time to start this. He glanced again at the clock and saw they had thirty seconds to go.

He quickly threw off his clothes and shifted. His muscles grew taut with every new growl or grunt from his pack members. There were very few others that presented a challenge to him. Tanner would be a nuisance and a few others lost in bloodlust would have to be neutralized, but all in all he had the best chance of reaching Kitty first.

The command to go erupted from his Alpha and Rafe took off at a dead run. He dove into the nearby woods and followed Kitty's strong scent in the exact direction he'd sent her. Good girl.

A few of the pack members flew by him and Rafe let them go. Clint and Charlie were no match for him and would lose steam long before anyone caught up with his wild cat. He also didn't believe that his allies in the pack were going to pursue her very hard. Pissing off the rising alpha could be a very tragic mistake if they weren't careful.

From the corner of his eye Rafe caught sight of Tanner and his two closest friends. They would not hesitate in their pursuit to support his foe. And while the rest of the pack had torn out of the barn like they were trying to escape the fiery gates of hell, this asshole had stuck to him like glue instead of forging his own path. It was clear he suspected that Kitty and he had a plan and Tanner wanted to make sure neither of them got away from him.

*Come on, asshole. Bring it on. I want you to follow me so when the time comes I can grind your ass into the ground until you beg for mercy.*

First he'd have to take care of his buddies. Rafe broke off the path he'd been running on and took a hard left in a different direction. The wind ruffled his fur and the scent of blooming wildflowers and various wildlife suddenly assaulted his senses. He'd been so focused on his mate's scent he'd missed out on the usual delights of a full moon hunt.

Now he was hoping his change of direction and the fading scent from Kitty would serve as the distraction he needed. Tanner's big blond friend, Alric, followed him the closest. The white fur of his wolf stood out well in the inky darkness of the dense tree cover and made him the perfect candidate for his first target.

Rafe came to a sudden stop and turned toward the man behind him with his jaws open. The surprising move made the other wolf's eyes widen but his body didn't react as quickly as his brain. Rafe grabbed onto one of Alric's legs with his mouth and clamped his teeth around the limb like an unstoppable vice. Flesh tore and blood gushed in Rafe's mouth seconds before the satisfying crunch of his opponent's bones gave way under the immense pressure. With one final grind to ensure the damage would last for at least several days, Rafe tore free and spun away.

Tanner stood nearby but had made no move to protect his friend. Rafe should have been surprised but he wasn't. These wolves were new to the pack and thus far had not demonstrated the same level of protectiveness towards anyone other than themselves. They'd remained distant and displayed more than their fair share of aggressiveness toward the females. Shortage of women or not, pack treasured their women.

Rafe growled. Tanner might be more alpha than beta, but he still had to fight for a higher rank in the pack and if he thought catching Kitty or removing him from the equation was even a remote possibility he had another thing coming. One aggressive move, and Rafe had the right to exert natural law. Tanner thought he had as much alpha in him as Rafe and he couldn't be more wrong. From day one he'd sensed the other man's restlessness but that didn't mean the same thing. His human half had a problem with authority, but in the right situation and after a proper ass kicking, his wolf would submit.

He probably should have taken the fact that Tanner stood at a distance watching as a sign of trouble but he wasn't thinking at one hundred percent knowing Kitty still ran alone and frightened. His only warning was the sudden rush of air behind him and ear-splitting howl of Tanner's other friend a second before he landed on Rafe's back. Rafe dropped to the ground and rolled to his side, dislodging the other wolf's claws that had begun to dig into his hide.

Rafe slashed to his side, catching the rear haunch of the enraged wolf before he could move out of the way. The wolf scrambled to the side in attempt to knock him loose. Rafe dug deeper and wrapped his other leg around the animal's body. With the wolf wrapped in his embrace, he bent forward and clamped his fangs around the vulnerable throat. The wolf immediately stilled and began to whine. Game over. Rafe bit down enough to pierce the flesh and waited for the final show of submission from the other man.

The animal in Rafe really wanted to rip the throat from his quarry. Every second he held on to the wolf the more he wanted to sate the blood thirst rising inside him. The other man had attacked and he'd no doubt be justified. Except he didn't have time for the political fall out later. He needed to end this and get to Kitty.

Rafe flexed his front legs and extended his claws, making them dig deeper into the other wolf's hide. The scent of blood and fear filled the air around them. Another quarter inch and he'd hit the mother lode of arterial blood. It would be so easy and final...

The wolf underneath him must have sensed what was about to happen. He whined and the familiar magic of a shapeshifter shimmered in the air seconds before the wolf turned into a man. Submission granted. With renewed focus, Rafe scrambled off his opponent and growled. He turned and faced Tanner still waiting in the same spot near a clump of trees. Rafe caught his next opponent's gaze. They were both playing a game and they knew it. He guessed Tanner wanted him to use up his strength so that when the time came for the important fight it would be an easy task for him to take Rafe down.

Rafe panted for breath. While true having to eliminate Tanner's allies did take some of his strength, it gave Rafe a clear path to the other wolf. Their gazes were still locked, their muscles frozen in place until the sound of another wolf approaching set them both in motion. Tanner took off first and in the original direction Kitty had taken. The bastard knew she'd run for the neutral zone. Which is why he'd sent Kitty in a more circuitous route to her destination.

With a renewed sense of energy, he dug into the loosened earth and took off for the rendezvous point he'd arranged for them. It wasn't too far off the path that Tanner had taken so Rafe put every bit of energy into his speed and sent out a thanks to his little brothers for making him chaperone their many camping trips. Thanks to them he knew every inch of this forest frontward and backward twenty times over. Unlike a lot of the pack who preferred to live in town and only hunt on the full moon, his family favored the peace and serenity that came from nature.

Now he just had to find her before that bastard did.

# CHAPTER
# FOURTEEN

Kitty slowed to a stop when she reached the small creek that separated wolf territory from the neutral zone. She struggled to catch her breath. She had no idea how long she'd been running, only that her fight or flee instinct made her keep going. She could return to the house Kane had given her and hope for the best. Yet, something stopped her—pulled her back. That God damned mating bullshit.

She'd managed to jump from one frying pan to the next and Rafe wasn't making it easy for her to escape. He'd rescued her, taken her in, cared for her and even claimed her as his despite the baggage she came with. Why didn't he want to let her go like everyone else? She desperately wanted to chalk it all up to their DNA and be done with it. Until she remembered all the little things. He'd talked to her when they both thought she was dying and she'd clung to his voice. He'd been her lifeline.

There was a lot she didn't know about his plans for his pack but she felt it to her bones that, just like Simon said, he was destined for greatness. The last thing he needed was a scarred woman holding him back. Except she wouldn't leave it like this. She looked up at the giant oak tree that straddled the treaty lines. She'd wait for him so they could settle this between them once and for all. The cat yowled in her head. Her heart ached from being this far from her mate.

"We can't," she whispered, hoping eventually the longing would dissipate.

Kitty lifted her body upright and landed her two front paws on the tree trunk. Her claws flexed and dug into the bark as she prepared to jump for the low lying branch.

The cat scented him first and turned on a scream. Her wolf emerged from the tree cover fifty yards away at a dead run. He didn't stop or slow, he simply slammed into her and pinned her to the tree. Kitty snarled and scraped at the bark.

"Shift!" he commanded. She barely made out the word as the magic shimmered around them. They both changed at the same time and one minute she was pinned by an angry wolf and the next she was skin to skin with the man who wouldn't let her go. There was nothing left to do except succumb.

"I need you." He laved the side of her neck with his tongue. The scent of sweat and earth and man surrounded her.

"Oh, hell," she moaned, her need just as obvious as his. How was she supposed to deny him anything?

"Has to be now. I can't wait." His teeth grazed the same path his tongue had taken sending shivers shooting up and down her spine.

"Yes," she breathed, unable to stop the moan that followed.

His hands roamed her sides, the rough skin giving her tingles everywhere he touched. His hand cupped the side of her breast and he raked over her nipple. Oh damn.

Her fingers flexed and her feline claws grasped at the tree. Without his support she'd fall to her knees. The hard, corded muscle of his chest pressed into her back. The current running between them arced as the burning inside her grew to an impossible level.

In that moment her awareness dawned. No matter what happened, whether she stayed with him or not, nothing would ever be enough when it came to him. She'd crave him constantly. Her thoughts scattered when calloused fingers trailed down her side and between her legs. What could she say that her wetness hadn't already told him? Still her body stretched and her back arched into his touch. She definitely had to have more.

She felt the hot, rigid length of his erection pressed to her backside, dipping lower and lower...

"Tell me you want this too," he growled. "That you'll stay and we'll do this together."

Before she could answer, Rafe was ripped away from her.

"She's mine, asshole."

Her head whipped around. Shit. Tanner had found them and he'd caught Rafe in the worst possible moment.

"No," she cried.

To her surprise, Rafe recovered quickly. He shook his head once and ran at the shithead who'd attacked him, shifting into a giant half wolf half man as he did. In a blur of movement the fight became a whirlwind of teeth, claws, and hair. Tanner's darker wolf didn't look like he stood a chance against Rafe's bigger body. Except the bastard's gaze was filled with so much rage it propelled him to be a more matched opponent.

Kitty yelled for Rafe until her throat ached as they tore into each other's hides, legs and shoulders. Her mate had as much anger going for him as Tanner did with the added adrenalin of protecting her. Every time the darker wolf pounced on him, Rafe kicked him off.

"Face it, Tanner. You lost her fair and square. She's my mate and you can't have her."

"Mate? Seriously? You'd mate with that?" He pointed to her and the blood drained from her face. He didn't say it but between being a feline and damaged goods, he thought Rafe had to be insane.

Kitty watched Rafe's features change. This time the human became part of the beast before he ran at the other man.

"Rafe stop!" She tried but neither man heard her. Wolf teeth tore into Tanner's side and blood filled Rafe's mouth. Tanner pushed back and they both tumbled through the trees and out of her view.

She had to stop this. She started to go to them and a big hand grabbed her wound-free arm. "You can't intervene."

"But they'll kill each other." She turned to the stranger and blinked up at the man now towering over her, shoulders so broad he blotted out the moonlight behind him. His brilliant yellow eyes were fixed on her, as if nothing out of the ordinary took place behind her. His T-shirt, jeans and shit kicker boots might have appeared casual bad boy to most but there was nothing remotely casual about the grip wrapped around her arm or the power wielded in his eyes.

"Name's Bhric. And if I'm not mistaken, you belong to me."

Kitty yanked at her arm in an attempt to get free and nothing happened. Finally, she sighed. "Why in the world does everyone all of a sudden have claim to me? I'm a feline shifter, not some goddamn chew toy for everyone to fight over. I don't belong to you at all."

He flipped her arm over and pointed at the small symbol inked into her wrist. "This says differently."

Well, fuck. She vaguely remembered being told she had to report in to the leader at the Dark Moon bar on the edge of the neutral zone. But so much had happened, she'd obviously forgotten.

"You're in charge of—?"

"Yep. I'm the one who corrals all the misfits and rejects. And once I got word about you being found here, I knew I'd have to round you up eventually."

"I take it back. I'm not a chew toy to you. I'm cattle. Even better."

"Look. As much fun as this is, we don't have much time before one of them comes looking for you and this happens to be my favorite shirt. I don't care to ruin it today."

Kitty blinked at him and stared at the plain white T-shirt. Was he for real? "I'm supposed to come with you, just like that?"

His face split into an odd grin. "If you're feeling kind of shy, you can always shift and follow me."

She looked down at her nudity and shrugged. It's not as if it had ever bothered her before. But the thought of leaving Rafe in the middle of his fight to save her didn't sit well at all. "Do I have a choice?" she asked.

His face grew serious once again and his eyebrows drew together. "There is always a choice to be made, Kitty of Clan Gunn, but I don't believe in making you do so under duress. If either of these wolves wants to stake a claim they can do so on my land. Then you can make your choice. Not here."

She simply stared, shell shocked by the validity of his easy statement.

"Come." He tugged on her arm and she gave in to the urge to escape. She wasn't sure the neutral zone meant freedom, but it felt a lot more stable than the woods where wolves were currently hunting her and a man who'd do anything to keep her.

# CHAPTER
# FIFTEEN

Bhric pulled his jeep into the back parking lot of an old wood two-story building nestled on the edge of the forest and Kitty got her first look at the infamous Dark Moon. It kind of reminded her of an old time saloon except instead of horses tied up front, there was a row of bad ass looking bikes in every size and shape. "This your place?" she asked.

"Yep. My father passed it on to me before he decided to retire to Florida." They both climbed from the jeep and Kitty had to stretch her legs to keep up with the giant strides of the hybrid in front of her.

"Your father left the Dragon?" It was so rare anyone of their kind ventured outside the region, it always made her curious.

He turned back to her. "Sweetheart, there's a big ole world out there and it's not as dangerous for a shifter as you might think. All it takes is some street smarts and a few well placed friends and you can fit right in."

"Then why do people like— I mean hybrids stay here? Why not go out into that big *ole* world as you call it?"

"Because people like me enjoy roots and tradition just like the rest of you. This is my home and I'm not about to be driven out because I'm not some pure blood wolf or feline. I'd rather serve as a constant reminder to assholes like your— I mean to the councils that we're here to stay so they might as well get over it."

He opened the front door and held it. "After you, my lady."

She winced at the obvious sarcasm and a twinge of guilt fluttered inside her. "I really didn't mean to offend you. I'm in no position to judge, but I'm still curious about the people I'm supposed to live with."

"Oh trust me, you are not the first to show up at my doorstep with questions and a lot of bad information. That's the problem with these councils. They still program their people to believe in the old ways."

Kitty stepped into the bar and felt a sudden sense of déjà vu. Or maybe she'd simply been thrown back in time. Classic rock played on some unseen stereo system and dark wood was everywhere. On the floors, on the walls, even on the bar. A smattering of tables and chairs covered some of the space in front of her with a few people sitting at them eating something that smelled—she sniffed the air and tried to decipher the scents—delicious actually.

In the far corner of the room she spotted two pool tables set up and that's where most of the patrons had gathered.

"Pool tournament tonight. They'll be at it for hours." Bhric must have followed her gaze. "Let me introduce you to a couple of people you'll need to know."

He steered her in the direction of the bar and the very good looking man tending it. "This here is

Greer, I guess you could say he's my right hand man."

"Right hand, left hand, brain. Whatever." Greer greeted her with a large smile. "You must be Kitty. We've been hearing a lot about you the last few days."

She felt her eyebrows rise as she shook the hand offered to her. "Do I even want to know?"

He snorted. "Probably not. You're probably better off not knowing how much gossip goes on when a cat wanders into the wolf barn on accident."

Kitty's cougar snapped to attention and yowled inside her head. "Well, you should probably inform your people that I did not wander over there by accident."

Bhric took a seat on the stool next to where she stood. "Exactly, and I think we need to discuss the details about what happened."

Kitty turned her head away. "No. I'm not interested in payback."

"Payback? How about justice?" Greer interjected.

"Justice has been served. Now it's time to move on. Do you have a bathroom in this establishment that I could use? Maybe grab a shower?"

"Sure, there is an employee area behind the kitchen that should work. But you should know that Kane has already been here looking for you. He took the evidence Nikki gathered and I imagine he'll deal with the women who attacked you whether you like it or not."

Kitty shrugged. She didn't care if Kane played disgruntled big brother and watched her back. There was only one man she cared about. "Whatever," she said. "Can I get my shower now?"

"Sure. I'll send someone over to your place and grab some of your clothes."

She swiveled toward Bhric. "I never got the chance to even put anything in that place. Everything is still in my car."

"Nah. When I sent Nikki over there to investigate she took the liberty of putting your stuff in the house and locking your car in the garage."

She sighed. "I guess I owe a thanks to this Nikki then." Although the thought of going near that house again held no appeal. The attack she could get over. It was the fact that it wasn't Rafe's place that tore her up on the inside. Leaving him in the middle of a fight with Tanner had to have been the dumbest thing she'd ever agreed to. That's what her heart said. Her head on the other hand, still wanted her to do the right thing.

Kitty left and headed in the direction Greer had pointed out to her. She'd barely gotten out of eyesight when she overheard Bhric talking. "Better batten down the hatches. We're about to get a visit from one very pissed off wolf."

"Oh yeah? So those rumors are true too. He's mated her?"

"That's the part I don't get. Even though she reeks of him, she's not marked."

"Huh," Greer responded. "I thought nature won no matter what in the case of born mates. Maybe that means it's not as serious as the gossipers have implied."

"Don't count on that. The tension is so strong between them it nearly took me to my knees."

"Oh, great. And he's coming here. Are you sure?"

Kitty sped up and got out of earshot before Bhric said another word. The last thing she needed to rely on now was some trumped up hope. She found the bathroom door and pushed inside and came face to face with a fair skinned curvy blonde with hair so light it almost looked white and pale blue eyes like she'd never seen before. They looked like they were glowing. Goosebumps rose on her skin and the hair on the back of her neck stood on end.

"I'm sorry but you can't be back here. Employees only," the woman said.

Kitty stood rooted to the spot and continued to stare. She'd never seen one of her kind before and she couldn't stop studying her.

"What?" the woman demanded.

"I've—I've never seen— I mean— I— Sorry." Obviously her ability to talk coherently had left the building.

"Yeah. I could say the same thing. I've never seen anything like you either. Is that what those women did to you?"

"How did you..." Oh, this had to be Nikki, the woman Bhric had mentioned. He'd sent a white cougar to investigate? "Are you—"

"Yes, I have white fur. I'm one of *those*."

Kitty shook her head. "That's not what I meant. I got that part on my own. Are you pregnant?"

The woman in front of her froze. Her muscles in her jaw clenched and hands balled into fists.

Kitty took a step back.

"What made you say that?" The question came out on a deep throated growl.

"I—I don't know. I just kind of saw it."

The now angry woman tilted her head and stared down at her own belly. "That's impossible. I'm not even showing yet."

"Look. I didn't mean to make you uncomfortable, but you're in a bar with shifters. You don't think they're going to scent it?"

"You're the first one who has. You're also the first one who's nosed into my business."

Kitty raised her hands in surrender. "I just came back here for a shower. Bhric said it was okay. I don't know anything about you or your business."

The woman stared at her for a few uncomfortable seconds before she relaxed. "It's all yours. But keep your nose out from where it most definitely does not belong. My body is private, got it?"

Kitty nodded her head. "Got it." The other woman left and Kitty exhaled a breath of relief. Shifters in general could be defensive and edgy about their private affairs but one best known for her assassination skills took that to a whole new level. She was starting to think living a sheltered life hadn't been all bad.

As had become the norm for several days now, her thoughts turned to Rafe. She had no doubt that he'd defeated Tanner and she had no doubt he was pissed when he found her gone. But dammit. She had to believe leaving him was the best thing. If Bhric was right though, and he was headed her way, she wasn't sure she could say no again.

Kitty lifted her head and checked the room. Lockers across one wall, none with any kind of lock system on them, a few chairs and benches for sitting and dressing, and an open doorway across the room that had to lead to the bathroom. That's where she needed to be. It was time to see what everyone else did.

She crossed the room and stopped at the sink. Her stomach churned with nervous acid at the thought of seeing her damaged face. "Suck it up, crybaby." She lifted her head and stared at her reflection.

Her heart squeezed and the air was sucked from her lungs on a strangled cry.

While the right side of her face remained smooth and untouched, the left side was a mangled, disgusting mess. Three long, deep scars from just below her eye to nearly her mouth remained from the fight. Ugly marks. She ran her fingers from top to bottom across the uneven, rippled flesh. Her stomach curled at the hideous sensation. How did anyone tolerate looking at her? Anger, so hot it nearly scalded her insides, flared to life. She couldn't stand to look at it for another second. In a lightning fast move, her fist connected with the reflective glass and it splintered in every direction.

Part of her wanted to scream in outrage at what had been done to her. The severity of her wounds would serve as a reminder every day of the person she used to be. She didn't exactly know what came next for her, but she wanted to find out. The hatred and intolerance that had festered inside her father and turned him into a monster could have done the very same thing to her if this had not happened. Kitty's back stiffened and her chin raised. Then there was the matter of the wolf who may or may not be coming after her.

Her body softened as the emotions his presence created were resurrected. Was she really willing to walk away from him if it meant either of them would suffer for the rest of their lives? Bhric had promised her she had a choice and that reason had been the only one that had gotten her to leave with him. Away from Rafe, she still ached for him. Would time ease that loss for her? She pushed her hands through her hair and slammed her elbows on the porcelain sink at her waist. There were too many unanswered questions for her to rifle through.

She lifted her head. "Do you love him?" she asked her cracked reflection. Of course she did. Whether she knew him for one week or one year would make no difference. But what he deserved and what she wanted were two entirely different things.

## CHAPTER
# SIXTEEN

Rafe stared at the front door of Dark Moon in his wolf form and shifted. It'd be a little hard to tear the door off its hinges without his hands. And tear the place down he was about to do. Bhric had gone too far taking his mate away without even talking to him. A snatch and grab in the middle of a dominance fight was a damned dirty trick.

He yanked on the handle with a good portion of his wolf strength and pulled the door from its frame. Just inside three wolves stood side by side blocking his entry.

"Rafe. Nice to see you again."

"Fuck you, Greer. Where's my mate?" He glanced over their shoulders and searched the area he could see. No Kitty.

"First, you need to put on these." Greer handed him a pair of jeans and a T-shirt. "You're lucky we heard you coming. Storming in here buck ass naked and stirring up every shifter and human inside is not how you want to approach Bhric about getting your kitty cat returned."

Rafe growled, but grabbed the jeans. He didn't give a shit about clothes but he had enough wits still about him to know Bhric could keep him from her for a while if he wanted to. So he shoved his legs in the pants and threw the shirt over his head. "Now where is she?" He'd already scented her outside and it was driving him crazy.

"First you talk to Bhric. You of all people know the deal here." Greer broke off from the other two and headed back inside. Rafe followed. The half wolf led him to Bhric's office where a giant of a man stood watch at the door. He sniffed. "Is that a—?"

"Bear?" Greer finished. "Sure is. Rafe meet Calder, our latest resident to join the fold."

Calder the seven-foot bear grunted a greeting but didn't uncross his arms from his chest or step aside.

"Since when does Bhric need a bodyguard?"

Greer sneered. "You might not want to say that too loud. Calder here is our new security team for the bar. He overheard you were coming in hot and bloodthirsty and he wanted to greet your personally."

The big bear grunted again at the same time the door opened and Bhric emerged from his office.

"That took you a lot longer than I expected."

"I want my mate," Rafe growled. He was too ramped up from the fight with Tanner to play these waiting games.

"Ahh. Fine. Let's skip the chit chat. I'm afraid the real question is... Does she want you?"

"We're mates. Of course she does."

"Then why isn't she marked yet?" Bhric lifted a brow with the question.

"We've been a little distracted, what with her getting attacked here in your territory, her almost dying from whatever they poisoned her with and then Tanner deciding he had rights that somehow trumped mine. So it's been a hell of a week, but if she'll accept me I plan to make it official as soon as possible."

Bhric stared at him long and hard. The man had an incredible amount of power, but Rafe would do whatever it took to get Kitty back. When he'd discovered her missing his wolf had gone into a frenzy until he was able to pick up Bhric's scent. At least then he'd known she was safe and not stolen by someone wanting to hurt her or him. At that point he should have reported in to Burke to give him a situation report, but instead he headed here. Before Tanner had interrupted they'd started the mating process and unless Kitty outright refused they were damn well going to finish it tonight.

"I guess you should go and see your mate then. But know this. The whole reason I brought her here was so I made sure she knew *all* of her choices. Yes, ignoring the mating call is hard and often painful, but it can be done when it's for the right reason."

Rafe nodded and walked away. There was nothing else to say to anyone other than Kitty. He followed her scent and as he got near it changed. Something was wrong. His wolf howled in fear as he sprinted to the back of the building. He shoved through a door marked *employees only* and searched the room. Nothing there, but her scent was stronger. The sound of running water from another room drew his attention and he raced inside. The first thing he noticed was the broken mirror. Oh shit. He'd forgotten all about the fact she hadn't seen her face yet. Dammit.

This close he could hear her tears and they damn near gutted him. There was nothing more that he wanted in this world right now than to take her pain away. He forced himself to stay calm and not scare her.

"Kitty."

The soft cries stopped and he heard nothing except the water. She was holding her breath. He undressed and slid the curtain to the side. His heart broke when he found her sitting in the corner with her legs pulled tight to her chest. The sadness written all over her face undid him. "Please don't cry, baby." He squatted next to her and touched her scarred cheek. "These scars are nothing. I knew the moment I found you in the clearing looking half dead you were the most beautiful creature I'd ever seen. You. Are. Perfect."

"I'm not perfect," she said. "I've done awful things."

"And that's what makes you so damned great. Yes, you've made mistakes, but you also learned from them. Do you realize that since you've gained your freedom, you've done everything you could for me?"

She blinked at him. "I don't know. I haven't exactly been free. I feel like I've been fighting for my life since I left the clan."

He couldn't stand not having her in his arms any longer so he sat next to her and lifted her into his lap. Her cougar heat felt so good against his skin. He wrapped his arms around her and got as close as he could.

"You have. But in that time you found me. That's got to count for something." He pressed his lips to the base of her neck and then scraped his canines along the tender skin.

She wiggled in his lap. "Maybe."

"Maybe nothing. If that bastard Tanner hadn't interrupted us, our mating would be official."

She swiveled in his lap. "What happened with Tanner? Is he dead?"

"No, he's not. He fought hard as hell for a while but he gave in and submitted when he believed his death was imminent."

"So you'll be the alpha?"

"Are cats always this chatty when naked in the shower? Enough talk." It was too hard to keep up this line of conversation with an aroused goddess wiggling around in his lap, teasing him. "I want my mate."

"Oh, Rafe." She softly touched her lips to his. "I want what I can't have so bad."

Rafe threaded his fingers into her wet hair and tugged her head back until their gazes met. "You and I are going to have a long talk after this. Can't is no longer an option. But right now thinking is impossible."

"Everyone will hear us."

They would. Shifters and their sensitive hearing needed sound proof rooms for any kind of privacy and he doubted this old building had sound proof anything. "Oh well," he replied and tightened his grip on her.

Her lips drifted past his lips and along his jaw. The power of the mating call was so damned strong in them both, but he sensed her resistance. Her attempt to deny it wasn't going to last much longer. He hoped.

She slid her hands to the side of his neck and her thumbs stroked over his pulse. Oh yeah. Her head might still be in some sort of fight, but the animal inside her knew exactly what it wanted. Rafe grabbed her around the waist and twisted her until she fully faced him with her bare sex hovering over his pulsing cock.

"One of these days we're going to do this in slow motion. But not today." He kissed her hard with a hunger that more than matched hers. He'd never felt so starved in his whole life and only this woman could satiate him. His tongue pushed between her lips as the spiced taste of wild woman filled his head. It reminded him of the forest after a hard summer rain, where the steam from the ground made everything around him more vibrant and alive.

Power coursed through his veins until her hand slipped between their bodies and wrapped around his rigid erection. Then his vision darkened and all he could see or feel was the wonder of his mate touching him. Good God, she felt incredible. She caressed him with slow, easy strokes that were either going to kill him or make him explode. For a brief second her slick heat touched him and his brain melted a bit more. He growled for more.

"Not yet," she whispered. Before he could protest, she slid from his lap, knelt in front of him and licked his shaft from the bottom to the top like a damned lollipop. She stared up at him with such heat in her gaze he could barely breathe. He slammed his head against the wall. "Fucking hell."

She responded by drawing his full length inside her mouth and sucking hard. His hips shot from the ground and his hand tightened on her hair. "Damn, woman. You're mouth. Holy..."

Kitty smiled around his dick and did it again, this time nearly blowing off his head. Seriously. She was going to kill him. He'd give her anything in the world she wanted if she promised to never stop. Her tongue lashed across the underside and her hand reached for his balls. He was going to explode and ruin everything if he didn't stop her. He lifted her off of him and laid her out across the shower floor. Water pelted both their bodies and neither of them cared.

"My turn, bad kitty." He pushed his hands between her legs and spread them wide, taking a good long look. He stared up at her as he pressed a kiss to the top of her mound. Her small whimper delighted him. Turnabout was definitely fair play. He slid his hands along her curvy hips and torso before cupping her breasts. They more than filled his hands and he imagined spending hours playing with them, among other filthy ideas he'd have to show her. He followed his hands with his mouth and licked at her nipples until the tight peaks stood tall and tight. The more he touched and tasted the hungrier he grew. His need to devour her drove him wild.

It wasn't until his mouth hovered over her sex that Kitty began to beg. Heat rose from her body and he licked his lips in anticipation. "I've been waiting a long time for this," he growled. Rafe swiped his tongue through her wet center, making sure to avoid a certain hot spot he knew ached by now.

"Oh my God, more," she said. "More."

Her demand unleashed a wave of possessiveness he tried to hold back. Her legs tightened to grip his shoulders as he did everything in his power to drive her as far over the edge as him. She writhed and cried out until they were both mindless with pleasure. Only then did he circle her clit very slowly before wrapping his lips around it and sucking it into his mouth. This time the cougar screamed and he imagined the entire room shaking from his mate's overwhelming pleasure.

He lifted his head and pressed her thighs open with a tight grip on each leg. He lined himself up and stared into her eyes as the tip sank forward. He hesitated and let her sweet moan wash over him.

"Stop torturing me," she cried.

"My pleasure," he said and slid deep. Her mouth opened and no sound came out, but the perfect little O of her mouth and the widening of her eyes made him smile. Where he found the control to tease her he had no idea. Her tight sheath squeezed and pulled with the slightest movement and all he thought about was making her beg some more. He lifted her from the hard floor and she wrapped her legs around his waist. His hips flexed and he worked even deeper while keeping the pace insanely slow.

The deliberate drag of her heat along his length made them both moan at the agonizing pleasure.

"More, Rafe. Please. You're killing me."

For a second all he could focus on was the golden glow of her eyes as the animal drew closer to the surface. That look pleaded with him to do whatever was necessary to make her his. His teeth ached with the need to bite her. His heart knew that she cared for him and if he claimed her now she'd accept it. Eventually. His lips curled back and his gaze moved from her face to her neck. He had to. He couldn't.

Fuck that. His wolf wanted control. No. He clamped his mouth shut and resisted the urge with everything he had.

Kitty wrapped her arms around his neck and pulled him close so her lips were against his ear. "Love me, Rafe. Just love me."

Rafe broke, driving his cock deeper than before. This time he didn't stop. Thrust after thrust he filled her, each one more intense than the last. His hands were gripped roughly at her waist but he couldn't stop. Lust raged inside him, completely out of control. Her eyes closed and she appeared as lost as he in the driving sensations. He leaned forward and took one of her hardened nipples between his front teeth. If he couldn't mark her in the way he wanted, this would be the next best thing. He bit down hard until she grabbed his hair and cried out. Her sex tightened mercilessly around his cock, forcing him deeper inside her.

Loving her reaction, he lifted his hips up and over changing the angle of his deep, penetrating thrusts. The plan had been to drive her mindless and instead his body tingled with so much savage pleasure he couldn't stop.

"Harder," she begged. "Oh shit. So close."

"I'll give you anything. Anything you want," he promised as he leaned forward and took her mouth with a brutal kiss. Together they bucked and thrust, trying to get closer than ever before, as if bound together with or without their mate marks. When the storm threatening them both finally broke free, Kitty threw her head back and screamed. High pitched and loud, the sound tore into his control and pulled him straight into the white-hot center of a burning orgasm. Together they jerked and tumbled to the floor, Rafe rolled, catching Kitty before she hit the hard tile. She shuddered in his arms as the aftershocks rocked through them.

Her head rested on his shoulder in silence as their heart beats slowed and their breathing returned to normal. He liked this a lot. Companionable silence where neither of them needed to talk so much as they simply wanted to be held. He didn't have to hear the words to know that she still had her doubts. He was okay with that for now. Very soon she would realize that he had enough power and confidence for them both.

～

"You owe me five hundred bucks." Bhric filled the bathroom doorway and glared down at them.

Neither Kitty nor Rafe moved. Shifters weren't exactly shy about sex and they'd nearly killed themselves with pleasure in a bout in the shower. Whatever Bhric wanted he'd have to face them as they were. Naked and exhausted.

"And why would I owe you any money at all?"

"Because you sent my entire bar into a frenzy. The walls are paper thin in this old building and her screams made it impossible for them to think about playing pool or drinking my liquor. They couldn't get out of here fast enough to go find someone to fuck."

"Oh no! Your pool tournament." Kitty buried her face in Rafe's shoulder and giggled. Obviously she knew more than he did about Bhric's ramblings.

"Right. It's our best night of the week, so you owe me five hundred bucks for lost business."

Rafe thought about their predicament for a minute and shrugged. He didn't really care much about Bhric's business, but with Kitty by his side he had no reason to argue. She's made him a very happy man. "Whatever. It was worth every penny."

"Hey!" Kitty shoved at his arm and he tightened his protective hold around her waist.

Bhric or no Bhric, her feistiness was beginning to stir him again. Once had only temporarily satisfied him and soon he'd be ready for more. In fact, if he had his way they'd be at this all night.

"You two are bad for business. Either take it to her house or yours. I don't care. Just not in my bar again. Got it?"

Rafe smiled and a deeper respect for the leader Bhric had become settled in his mind. He'd meant what he'd said about Kitty making her own choices. He had a feeling that in the days and weeks to come he might find a powerful friend in the leader of the neutral zone.

"Sure. No problem." He stood and lifted Kitty into his arms. "It's time I take Kitty home where she belongs.

# CHAPTER
# SEVENTEEN

"So what now?" Rafe had explained to Kitty for the twentieth time in a week that he wasn't letting her go and so far she'd resisted the idea. Kind of. They'd been together day and night and she'd grown rather attached. However, their differences still worried her, especially in relation to his becoming the Alpha.

"Well, first we talk to Burke. The ceremony of transfer was supposed to take place tomorrow night, but after that stunt the bastard pulled in the barn, I don't know what he's thinking."

"That *bastard* was thinking his nephew needed to stand up to the pack and prove his worthiness. If I'd just handed her over to you with absolutely no regard for pack law, we'd be canceling that ceremony tomorrow and every wolf with an ounce of alpha would be calling you out for a challenge."

Both Rafe and Simon jumped to their feet at the sound of Burke's voice and Kitty almost burst out laughing. It amazed her that Burke had been able to sneak up on all three of them without them being the wiser, but she respected the man for his power and cunning this far. Even if he did sic Tanner on her that night.

All three men stared at each other and she got the feeling they were all waiting for someone to say something. She rolled her eyes. Enlightened or not, times like these where they struggled needlessly for someone to back down, killed her.

"Burke, please have a seat. We were just talking about you." She smiled sweetly.

"So I heard." He took a seat across from both men and crossed his ankle over his knee. "I thought you two were mates?" He swept a glance over both of them.

Kitty rolled her eyes again. "Is everyone going to ask us that every time we meet them?"

Rafe touched Kitty's hand and turned to Burke. "We are. It's just Kitty is being a tad stubborn about making it official and I promised Bhric it would be her choice."

"What's the problem?" Burke addressed the question to her.

Kitty choked down the automatic sarcasm that leapt to her tongue. If she was going to get a straight answer then she needed to act like a grown woman and not a petulant child.

"I can't stand the thought of holding him back."

"Kitty," Rafe warned.

"No, let her speak. I think she needs to get this out." Burke sat back in his chair and waited for her to continue.

"I just mean that it's clear Rafe would make a great Alpha and I can't stand the thought of him having to sacrifice that because of what I am."

"You think if he is mated to a cougar instead of a wolf, he'll be any less of a leader?"

Kitty glared at Burke. "Of course not. He doesn't discriminate against anyone. In fact, I've never met anyone else who would willing take on his whole pack just to rescue a stranger." She tried to hold back her anger but it was impossible to hide. "I've been around bigoted shapeshifters my whole life, and I know him mating with me will bring his cause a lot of extra resistance on all of his incredible ideas."

Burke silently stared at her for a few seconds before he shrugged and turned to his nephew. "She seems perfect to me. I can already imagine her kicking ass and taking names. I dare some of our pack to try and resist her."

"My sentiments exactly."

"See you tomorrow then?" Burke stood and held out his hand to Rafe.

"Yes." They shook hands and Burke disappeared the same way he arrived.

"What just happened?" Kitty looked between Rafe and Simon.

Simon grinned. "That's my cue to take my leave as well. Guess I'll see you two at sunset tommorrow. Try not to be late."

After Simon left, Kitty didn't know what to say. All of her valid reasoning for not mating with Rafe had apparently fallen on deaf ears.

"Are you done saying no yet?" he asked.

Her throat tightened at the simple question. The need building inside her since she'd met him threatened to explode. "I'm not sure I can wrap my head around everyone being so accepting."

"Not everyone will be, but everyone who matters is. Is there anything more important than that?"

"You're never going to listen to me are you?"

He lifted her hand to his lips. "Of course, I am. When you're right." He grinned a slow, wicked smile and leaned into her. "There's nothing right about not being my mate." Letting a claw extend, he sliced through one of the thin straps holding up her dress. "What's even more not right is you sitting over there while I'm over here."

He grabbed her around the waist and lifted her onto his lap facing him so she could straddle him. Using the same claw trick he slipped his hand under her dress and sliced through the delicate lace of her panties.

"Hey. I really liked those."

"Me too. That's why I'm going to order them in every color, every month so I can cut them off of you whenever I want."

*Oh hell.*

Rafe reached between them and tore at the fastener of his jeans and freed his thickening cock. Kitty settled her thighs on the outside of his legs until her sex rubbed right over his tip.

"You're so wet," he groaned.

"You're positive this is what you want?" she asked. Not that either of them could resist for much longer. Every time he got near her, his body gave off pheromones that made her want to bite him.

"Never been more sure in my life. From the moment I met you." He kissed the curve of her partially bared breast. "What kind of leader am I if I'm not willing to put my money where my mouth is?"

"Rafe. Stop talking." His teasing touches were driving her mad. Kitty dug her fingers into his shoulders as the rest of her sank down on him. Damn she loved how he filled her. She clenched her muscles around his thickness and watched his eyes roll back in his head. When he got his bearings again, he leaned down and sucked her nipple between his teeth and nipped her. She cried out, her hand grabbing at his hair with all of her strength. He growled and bared his neck. "Do it, Kitty. Make me yours forever."

"Only if you move." Her voice was shaky when she spoke.

"With pleasure." Rolling his hips, he began moving inside her. The instant friction set them both on fire as heat rose between them.

Kitty leaned forward and pressed her lips to Rafe's neck. The heady scent of musk and damp forest suffused her, growing stronger. He'd barely begun and she was already close.

"Now, Kitty."

He pumped his hips faster as she scraped his skin with her sharp, pointed teeth. She had no idea what real pleasure meant until she met Rafe. He drove deeper and the time for thinking ended. With one hand in his hair and her mouth latched to his neck she lifted and fell in rhythm as her body melted into pure sensation in his arms. She wanted more and he gave it to her, surging inside her as her body tightened. She jerked him closer and drove her teeth into his neck, holding him in place as she shattered around him.

Underneath her, Rafe was growling, his cock pulsing inside her as they fell, lost in mind numbing pleasure. When they collapsed in an exhausted heap, Kitty slid her teeth free and laved across his mating mark. He was hers now.

"Damn, that feels good.

"Mmmhmm," she purred.

"You can't take it back."

Kitty lifted her head. "Guess you're stuck with me." A deep rumbling in her chest followed her words.

"Are you purring?"

She nuzzled his neck and trying to get even closer. "Maybe, why?"

"Because my contented Kitty, it's my turn and I won't take no for an answer."

She wiggled in his lap and clenched her muscles around his already growing erection. "Why in the world would I ever say no?"

"Why indeed," he growled.

Her purring grew louder as Rafe trailed kisses along the most sensitive part of her neck. She'd found love in the most unlikely of places and he'd taught her that life held quite a few more surprises. Sure, they still had a lot to learn about each other, but plenty of time to start figuring it all out.

*Tomorrow.*

She screamed.

# EPILOGUE

Kitty came awake on a sharp gasp that burned her throat. She jackknifed into a sitting position, clutching her chest as she tried to catch her breath.

"What's wrong?" Rafe grabbed her arms and pulled her close. "Bad dream?"

She rubbed at her throat and shook her head. "I don't think so. I think something horrible has happened."

Kitty broke from his hold and sprang from the bed, heading straight for the closet. Rafe followed her. "What are you doing? What's going on?"

By the time he'd asked the question she'd already dressed and was currently shoving her feet into a pair of sneakers.

"It's Nikki. Something's wrong with her."

His face scrunched in confusion. "Who's Nikki?"

"The pregnant white cougar I ran into at Dark Moon." Kitty turned to her new official mate. "She warned me to stay out of her business but this is really serious, Rafe. I've got to do something."

"Hold on, babe. You're not making any sense. You saw a white cougar? At Dark Moon?"

"How am I not making sense when you're repeating what I said and it's exactly what happened?" She bent back down and tied the laces of her shoes. "Yes, she was in the employee area of the building when I went back to use the bathroom. We spoke only for a minute but I saw she was pregnant. Well, I didn't see see. She wasn't showing yet. I saw. In my head. Well, anyway I blurted it out and she told me in no uncertain terms to mind my own business and that her body was private and all that jazz. And then she was gone."

Rafe stared at her as if she'd grown a third head. "Why on earth didn't you tell me that you'd spoken with an assassin?"

"Get a grip, Rafe. It's not as if I was hiring her to do a job."

"I still think this is something I should have heard about before the middle of the night with you waking up in a panic. What are we going to do at three in the morning, anyway?"

Kitty paused. "I guess we call Bhric. He hired her to investigate my attack so he must know her. Do you think he could be the father of her baby? He would need to know what has happened."

Rafe grabbed her wrist and held her still. "That's my point. Through all this babbling about seeing things and meeting dangerous assassins, I still don't know what you are talking about. What has happened?"

Her eyes widened as her vision reappeared in her head a bit like a movie. "She's been taken!"

~

DEAR READER,

Thank you so much for reading!

**If you enjoyed this book please take a moment to help other readers discover it by leaving a review on your favorite retailer.**

**Just a few words and some stars really does help!**

**Ready for more Southern Shifters?** *Be Were*, the fifth in the series is now available and you can read a preview at the end of this book.

If you want more information on all of the books in my Southern Shifters series, you can find the full reading order and links at ElizaGayle.com

**Turn the page for an excerpt of *Be Were*, the next book in the Southern Shifter series!**

# BE WERE SNEAK PEEK

By Eliza Gayle
Copyright 2014
All Rights Reserved

**Book Description:**

Dean had a family once. Until tragedy and betrayal consumed them. Now he lives on his own terms keeping life simple and carefree. Then one night leads to one bite and he's forced back into a dangerous world that reminds him he's still as angry as ever and this time he's not leaving until he gets what he wants. Niki.

Niki Harris has lived a life of secrets and solitude with no interest in making a change. But an easy one night stand turns complicated and she finds herself marked. Now she has to decide, tell the sexy shifter with a possessive streak a mile wide she's pregnant and in danger or do what she's always done--run.

## Excerpt

Dean scrubbed at the scarred wooden bar and pretended not to notice the sudden pit in his stomach that felt like someone had hollowed him out. The air was sucked from the room by his latest arrival. He didn't have to turn to see who had entered his bar. Yet he still watched the tall, imposing figure approach from the corner of his eye. The last thing he needed to see today, or any day for that matter, was his brother, Bhric. Their last parting had not been all that amicable and Dean had expected many years to pass before they saw each other again. Not a mere two.

All night he'd been out of sorts as the hours dragged on, and a sense of foreboding left him strung tight and aching to shift. The moment he'd finally made last call, he'd sighed in relief. The beast inside him wanted free *and now*. His instincts were telling him something was wrong but so far nothing had happened to clue him in to what. Until Bhric walked in.

"We're closed for the night," Dean said.

"Good thing I'm not here for a drink then, *brother*."

Inwardly Dean winced at the exaggerated endearment, while managing to keep his features neutral. This wasn't going to be pleasant.

"There's nothing else here for you."

Bhric stopped directly in front of him and Dean caught his gaze. He tried to read the man he used to gladly call family and failed. They'd parted ways with so much bitterness and bad blood between them, it was all he saw when he looked at him.

A man who'd betrayed him by fucking his girlfriend and then not telling him shit until she turned up pregnant. Dean believed the baby was his from the beginning, but no one was sure. Until the day the bitch walked out announcing neither of them had fathered her baby.

"I didn't come here to ask anything of you if that's what you're thinking, bro."

"Stop calling me that."

"What? You think just because we had a stupid fight a couple of years ago it means we're not brothers anymore? That's fucked up."

"No, what's fucked up is you coming here in the first place. Last I checked hell has not frozen over and you're still not welcome in my bar." Dean turned his back on Bhric and started to wipe down the bottles of alcohol along the back shelf. The sooner he finished up here the sooner he could break free from whatever his brother wanted.

Looking at Bhric only made him remember their shitty past. Especially Brenda, his former girlfriend whose knife he still couldn't get out of his back.

"Well, you're in luck then. I didn't come here because I missed you nor do I have any desire to rehash our problems. I have news about your mate."

Dean jerked before going completely still. His mate. Dammit.

After weeks of searching for the elusive white cougar who'd invaded his mind and bed on Christmas Eve, only to walk out the next morning, he'd taken a break from the hunt. He'd come close many times, but the wily female remained just out of his reach at all times. She always anticipated his next move and recently she'd quit toying with him and the trail had gone cold.

He hated to admit he'd enjoyed their little catch me if you can type game but it was time to end it. He wanted her back in his bed—in his life. They didn't exactly have to obey the laws of nature every time she waved the mate flag, but the idea of finding "the one" intrigued him. Sex between them had been explosive and his thoughts were pretty much consumed by wanting inside her again. But he also wanted to know her. She'd already proven to be more than just a beautiful face and hot bod, he wanted to know more.

Now his brother had something to do with her and the beast inside him was about to break all the rules. This shit could not happen again.

Slowly he turned to look at his brother, his eyes narrowing and his lips curling back in a snarl. "What have you done to her?"

"So I was right. I knew she was yours the minute she came to me. I could barely scent it, but it was there."

*She came to him?* Dean lurched forward and grabbed Bhric by the collar and yanked him halfway across the bar. "I'm not playing games with you, dick. What happened?" The thought of his sibling with his nose anywhere near Niki threatened to send him over the edge. "I swear by the Goddess, I will kill you this time."

His brother raised his hands in surrender, a move that didn't fool Dean for a second. "I'm really not here to start a fight. This isn't like before. I want to help you."

Dean snorted. Fat goddamn chance. "Then tell me what's going on. Where is Niki? And why the hell were you smelling her?"

Bhric smiled. "Don't get your panties in a twist little brother. It wasn't like that. I simply have a better sense of smell than you."

Dean hissed, baring the animal's teeth that crowded his mouth.

"Okay, okay. No more jokes. She's gone missing. We have reason to believe she has been kidnapped."

"What?" Anger ripped through Dean bringing his beast to the forefront. His face changed, elongating into the box-like snout of his jaguar, his nails turned to claws and black hair rippled across his skin. "Why would someone kidnap her and who is 'we'?"

AVAILABLE NOW

# ALSO BY ELIZA GAYLE

WICKED

WANTED

FERAL

FIERCE

FURY

**Single titles:**

VAMPIRE AWAKENING

WITCH AND WERE

# Writing as E.M. Gayle

CONTEMPORARY ROMANCE

**Mafia Mayhem Duet Series:**

MERCILESS SINNER

SINNER TAKES ALL

WICKED BEAST

WILLING BEAUTY

BROKEN SAINT

FALLEN ANGEL

**Outlaw Justice Series:**

SAVAGE PROTECTOR

RECKLESS PAWN

RUTHLESS REDEMPTION

**Outlaw Justice: Sins of Wrath MC:**

CRUEL SAVIOR

SCORCHED KING

VICIOUS DEFENDER

**Purgatory Masters Series:**

TUCKER'S FALL

LEVI'S ULTIMATUM

MASON'S RULE

GABE'S OBSESSION

GABE'S RECKONING

**Purgatory Club:**

ROPED

WATCH ME

TEASED

BURN

BOTTOMS UP

HOLD ME CLOSE

**Pleasure Playground Series:**

PLAY WITH ME

POWER PLAY

**Single Title:**

TAMING BEAUTY

WICKED CHRISTMAS EVE

# About the Author

Eliza Gayle is the New York Times and USA Today bestselling author of over 25 paranormal romance books. (She also writes contemporary romance under the name E.M. Gayle) She lives on a small island in the Pacific Northwest and spends her days writing romance, wandering the beach, kayaking or trying to remodel something. (She blames the latter on her obsession with HGTV and Pinterest.)

Before her writing career began, she served in the Marine Corps and lived a crazy life of adventure. She may not be active in the military at the moment, but in her heart she will always be that girl who would do anything to protect our freedom. She also still suffers from wanderlust and is frequently found planning her next adventure or traveling with her husband, laptop and all.

*For more information*
www.elizagayle.com
eliza@elizagayle.com

Gypsy Ink Books
www.gypsyinkbooks.wordpress.com

This book is a work of fiction. The names, characters, places and incidents are products of the writer's imagination or have been used fictitiously and are not to be construed as real. Any resemblance to persons, living or dead, actual events, locales or organizations is entirely coincidental.

All Rights Are Reserved. No part of this may be used or reproduced in any manner whatsoever without written permission, except in the case of brief quotations embodied in critical articles and reviews.

Printed in Great Britain
by Amazon

39901504R00169